P9-DGR-304

P813n

A NUGGET OF GOLD

A Nugget of Gold

Maureen Pople

HENRY HOLT AND COMPANY • NEW YORK

First published in the United States in 1989 by
Henry Holt and Company, Inc., 115 West 18th Street,
New York, New York 10011.
Originally published in Australia under the title
Pelican Creek by University of Queensland Press.

Library of Congress Cataloging-in-Publication Data
Pople, Maureen
    A nugget of gold / Maureen Pople.
        p.   cm.
Summary: Alternate chapters narrate two intertwining stories—one
of a nineteenth-century teenage girl in the goldfields of Australia;
the other of a present-day teenager who, in a nugget of gold,
discovers a link with the past and the explanation to a mystery
surrounding the earlier girl's marriage.
    ISBN 0-8050-0984-1
    [1. Australia—Fiction.]   I. Title.
PZ7.P7955Nu   1989
[Fic]—dc19   88-13918

Henry Holt books are available at special discounts
for bulk purchases for sales promotions, premiums,
fund-raising, or educational use. Special editions
or book excerpts can also be created to specification.

    For details contact:

    Special Sales Director
    Henry Holt and Company, Inc.
    115 West 18th Street
    New York, New York 10011

First American Edition

Designed by Maryann Leffingwell
Printed in the United States of America
10 9 8 7 6 5 4 3 2 1

A NUGGET OF GOLD

Sally

THE hole was very deep and the bottom, when I hit it, was hard. Smooth and damp and cold, and very *very* hard.

I felt extremely shaken and sick but was able to move everything without rattling, so I guessed my bones were intact. Actually there was one part of my anatomy that I could now move *much* more easily than before; I felt around, and sure enough my brand-new jeans had split all the way down the back seam. The button had sprung at the front as well, so for the first time since I'd put them on I was able to breath freely. *Now,* completely ruined, they were comfortable.

I turned my head and the darkness lightened. I could see stars above me, surprisingly close considering how far I'd fallen, but I decided not to call for help just yet. It might do them good to worry about me for a while.

So I settled back in my damp cubbyhole, feeling like Alice when she followed the bustling White Rabbit into Wonderland.

Thinking of rabbits brought to mind other animals. Like dingoes—bats—rodents—reptiles.

I began to scream, quite heartily, for help.

They took their sweet time coming. I heard them chatting together as if they were just out for a stroll, taking the evening air, and when they did arrive, they all seemed to think it was a great joke to hear me bellowing. I thought for a while they were planning to leave me down there. There was certainly a long and scintillating debate on whether I was worth the trouble it would take to pull me up. Finally I managed to calm my screaming panic enough to put a feeble note into my voice.

"I don't want to be a nuisance," I quavered, "but I wonder if I could have injured something . . . somewhere . . . I feel . . . very peculiar . . . somehow."

That did the trick.

"Hey, she might . . . you know. Hey, hang in there, Sally, I'll fetch a rope. Hey, you guys, go easy on her. Right?"

"Hey, Davey, hey, good thinking," I whispered. "Please hurry," I gasped. Then, remembering my jeans, I added: "Please David . . . a blanket . . . so cold . . ."

"And bring the big flashlight," ordered Annie.

"And the coil of rope from the shed," called Cooper.

Then I could hear him thundering off back to the house, muttering to himself, "Rope, blanket, flashlight, blanket, rope, flashlight." I was relieved. David is always making lists for himself (and anyone else who'll stand for it), but the habit must work, because once a thing has been listed, he seldom forgets it.

The others were quiet. It would have suited them to leave me there and just come along every now and again to chivvy me a bit and perhaps throw me a crust. Now they were realizing that they might have an injured person on their hands, maybe even feeling some guilt, I hoped. But that would change; their feelings would turn to hilarity when they spotted the split in my jeans.

I might as well admit right now that I am a tiny bit overweight. I tend to pudginess. If I were a foot and a half taller I'd be just right according to the charts, but as it is I measure five feet two and a half inches and I'm sixteen years of age, so that may be as tall as I'll ever be. So yes, I'm fat. A bit. Exactly what I weigh is strictly my own affair, of course.

The silence from above was unnerving me.

"Are you still there?" I murmured, remembering to keep the note of suffering in my voice.

"Yeah, we're still here. You okay?" Annie did sound really concerned, at last. "David went for a rope or something to get you out with. Look, Sally, I'm sorry . . ."

But whether she was sorry for being such a swine to me or just sorry that I'd gone and fallen down the well and probably hurt myself, she didn't say. We could hear David lumbering back, and soon I was blinking in the white glare of the big flashlight on my face.

Thus brilliantly illuminated I must have looked bedraggled, muddy, and ludicrous, because they all staggered about up there and talked in strained tones, obviously stifling laughter. I was *so* pleased to be in a position to afford them so much mirth.

I was just about to tell them so when I saw something gleaming in the soft soil beside a big rock by my right leg. Then David moved and the reflection was gone.

"Put it back," I yelled. "The flashlight, put it back where it was, David. I think I've found a diamond down here."

"Clever!" Annie drawled. "Finding a diamond. Just think of all those miners wasting their time looking for gold, and it was *diamonds* they should have been searching for all the time!"

"Oh, lots of diamonds around here." Cooper could hardly speak for laughing. "Thick on the ground they are. I've noticed the cattle swallow so many they nearly choke."

"Moo," Annie croaked.

But dear old David took pity on me and waved the flashlight around until it found the stone again. There *was* something shining beside it, and in spite of their obvious disbelief it *could* be a diamond. But I was determined not to let them know what I'd found, so I put my hand over the spot and directed the flashlight to another part of the hole and pretended to search there.

"No," I agreed, "you're right, it's not a diamond, just an old bit of glass. Sorry."

Meanwhile my fingers were busy scrabbling in the soil, digging out the object that had glimmered at me. It felt, in the dark, like a mud-encrusted pebble. I slipped it quickly into the small front pocket of my jeans.

David had brought some rope, and he now carefully snaked it down to me. "Hey, Sally, tie that around your . . . under your arms, and we'll haul you up."

Of course, I couldn't knot the stupid rope. It was thick and rough and I just couldn't do it in the dark with slippery, mud-covered hands. Finally I had to admit it, and Annie was as lethal as usual.

"Oh, do pull yourself together, darling," she said. "If you stood up you could practically *walk* out of the silly shaft. We're all trying to help you, so try to help yourself a little, hmm?"

If I could reach the top of this "shaft" as you call it, the first thing I'd do would be to haul you in with me, *darling*, I thought. No, better still, I'll wait until I'm safely out, and then I shall hurl you down here headfirst and walk away whistling. Never to return.

The rope came down again, this time with a thick piece from the branch of a tree tied to its end. It hit me in the face as it arrived, and of course I yelled with fright, since they had omitted to shine the flashlight down with it and I had no idea what was attacking me. I was beginning to see some advantage in *not* being saved, particularly by this inept and unwilling group of rescuers.

At last I realized what they wanted me to do, so I stood up, grabbed the hunk of wood firmly—well, actually I sort of hung on to the wood with my elbows—and clung like a limpet to the rope with my hands and held my breath and tried to think slim as they hauled me up. Their grunting and groaning was quite unnecessary as well as being in particularly poor taste, I felt. I was pushing against the sides with my feet and trying as hard as I could to help. I was also praying like mad that the rope would bear the strain and that the branch wouldn't break and that none of the three heartless loonies up top would let go of the rope.

I was quite surprised when I finally felt the earth flatten before me. I had to claw at the grass and hold tight as I fell forward, because the other three let go as soon as my head appeared over the rim of the hole. They dropped the rope and collapsed in a heap, and we all lay there for quite a while, they laughing their silly heads off and gasping for breath, me wondering quietly whether there was in fact any injury I could claim that would give me a break for a few days without being sprung by a doctor's examination or an X-ray. I didn't know enough about anatomy to make up a plausible set of symptoms, so I decided to feel vaguely unwell for as long as I could without being specific about it.

I also groped for the blanket that David had flung on the ground, and managed to cover my embarrassment before they recovered their senses. Then stupid Cooper suggested they carry me back to the house.

"You take her legs and I'll get her by the shoulders, Dave, I think we'll be able to manage her."

Made me sound like one of his stupid sheep, and anyway I could just see myself, backside bumping on rocks and tussocks while they staggered along, grumbling about their heavy load.

"I'll walk, thank you," I stipulated with dignity, and

they both gave hearty sighs of relief. So we made our way across the stony paddock, the boys supporting a tottering me and Annie walking in front, shining the flashlight at our feet. I decided to exact no revenge right away; it seemed less urgent now that I was away from the spooky atmosphere of the hole. Besides, to be quite practical, I needed their help to make it back to the house.

They were much more sympathetic when we reached the hallway.

"Hell!" Cooper exclaimed "You *did* take a beating. We'd better telephone Dr. Chan."

"Hey, she might have broken every bone in her body for all we know." Young David was a great comfort when he tried.

Annie was more matter-of-fact. "Oh, do be sensible," she said. "She couldn't possibly walk if she'd broken any bones. You reckon you broke anything, Sal?"

I gladly admitted that nothing felt broken, and claimed bravely that a hot bath and a rest would probably fix me up.

"Yes, I really don't think there's much wrong with you," she agreed, a trifle too swiftly I felt. "It wasn't a big fall, you know. That hole can't be very deep."

It had been quite deep enough for me and would have been for her, I was sure, but I really felt too worn-out to argue, so I nodded and trundled along toward the bathroom, dragging my blanket behind me.

Annie ran me a steaming hot bath and even added some of her Christmas bath salts, which was quite a concession. The water here is so hard, you have to use a softener, but smelly bath salts was a luxury and I hadn't thought to bring any with me. I waited as long as I decently could for her to leave, but she settled herself on the loo and seemed prepared to be overseer while I bathed. Since we had on occasions shared the actual bathwater when we were little, it did seem a trifle coy to order her out of the room now. So I eased off my jeans while still keeping the blanket around me, then undressed normally, but with some pain, and slid into the wonderfully relaxing and exotically scented water.

"Hurt much?" she inquired.

Now that I was safely out of the hole (and those jeans), and enjoying the comfort of the bath, I was prepared to admit that I hardly hurt at all, and apart from a few scratches and the sure promise of a bruise or two, I was unscathed. Annie leaned down and picked up my discarded clothing. She tossed my underwear and T-shirt into the laundry basket in the corner, then turned her attention to my jeans.

"Better chuck these straight out, eh?" She wiggled her fingers, her whole hand in fact, through the gaping hole in the seat and we both laughed. I was glad the tension that had built up between us earlier was now easing. I really am quite fond of Annie—we've been friends for years—so I was about to agree to the suggestion when suddenly I remembered the odd-shaped lump I had found down the hole. If she fossicked for one more moment she was sure to find it, and I didn't feel ready to look stupid when she pulled out an old piece of rock. Or a lump of clay with a bit of glass stuck to it. I was sure now that it must be one or the other.

But of course, I was wrong. It was neither.

Ann

"HEY! Miss Importance!" She surely could not have been speaking to me, but I turned to look because the voice was coming from an unusual angle, behind and very much below my left shoulder.

"You tell your father he calls me his 'good woman' just once more and I guarantee he'll suffer for it. You hear me?"

She *was* speaking to me! And I had no idea of how to answer, because my father *did* have a habit of addressing everyone as his inferior, and so she had my sympathy. Also she was such a bright little doll of a woman that it was difficult to be angry with her.

"I'll tell him," I said, "but I can give you no hope that it will change him.

"Nah," she grinned, "you're probably right at that. Cheer-o, then." And she hitched up her skirts and began to walk away.

"Just a minute. Why 'Miss Importance'? *I* don't call you 'my good woman.' "

"Well, I dunno. You're a tall one all right, and you walk like you're carrying a book or something on your head, and you do talk real la-de-da. Still, I s'pose you're not so bad. Can't go blaming you for your dad, can we? Sorry, love."

Calling a person "love" is just as bad as calling them your "good woman", I feel, and I had a lot of worries on my mind, so I was tempted to take advantage of my superior height and flatten her beneath my boot—she was certainly small enough—but charitably I refrained and we parted. As we turned, I noticed that she had a tiny baby slung in a shawl on her back. That, with the old gray felt hat she wore, probably her husband's, and her diminutive size made her appear to be a remarkably odd person.

"Come along then, all of youse!" she bellowed, in a voice much bigger than herself, and from behind a tent nearby came running no less than six children, the oldest no more than ten years of age I would say. I was glad I hadn't crushed her. Seven motherless children would take a lot of looking after.

They call this village Pelican Creek, even though the brook that bends nearby has no such bird. No doubt the name was given by one of the wild crowd of madmen who came here to make their fortunes on the goldfields. I have never seen such a godforsaken town, and every day I long to be back in Bloomsbury, in my grandparents' commodious house behind the British Museum, with the bustle of carriages on properly cobbled streets and the chatter of clean and well-attired people passing our door. Were it not for the boy who works in the smithy, I would gladly leave tomorrow.

It seems he has not seen me yet, although I pass by (of necessity, of course) almost every day. There are many forges here, but his is the biggest and busiest by far. There is a large wooden sign above the entrance, and burned into the wood are the words BLACKSMITHING AND SHOEING FORGE WHEELWRIGHTING FARRIERING AND

COACH BUILDING, WM. RYAN, PROP. I always pause to look at the horses being attended to; I wonder they feel no pain as the shoes are hammered onto their poor hooves.

Today I observed the horses patiently shuffling there, the clang of the hammers on the hot metal, and the brawny muscles of the smithies as they worked. But Mr. Wm. Ryan, who is the most brawny of them all, caught my eye and waited with his great hammer held high, and I fanned my face with the end of my shawl, overcome by the heat from the furnaces (which was of course the reason I stopped to rest outside his wretched establishment), and hurried by.

I was on my way to obtain help for my mother. She sighs, coughs, is pale and listless, so I have left her resting in the hut. The sign above the chemist's shop is not encouraging. P. SLY it says, CHEMIST AND DRUGGIST, HORSE MEDICINES, TEETH EXTRACTED, AMERICAN TWIST TOBACCO, and finally, to my relief, PRESCRIPTIONS CAREFULLY DISPENSED. So Mr. Sly might help us, although I fear maybe not as willingly as he would were my poor mother a horse.

There was a young man being served at the counter with, of course, a bottle of horse liniment. I had seen him before in the general store, so I nodded politely when he turned and smiled at me. Then he departed, and Mr. Sly gave me his attention. He was most reluctant to prescribe for my mother and suggested that she see the doctor when he next came to town.

"And when will that be?" I asked, expecting an answer in days.

"Hard to say, miss. He was here a month gone. Maybe two, three months."

My shocked face must have aroused some pity, because he then suggested that we could take my mother to the town of Gulgong, some miles away, where another doctor had rooms. In the meantime he gave me some of his own patent elixir and wished my mother well.

I was reluctant to pass the smithy in case the watchful Wm. Ryan took it upon himself to pause and glare at me again. I do like a workman to keep to his work and not stop to gape at young women who are forced to walk past on their lawful way to their homes. He had his back to me, however, and a horse's fetlock across his knee. I think it was a fetlock; I know little of horses' anatomy, but this one was keeping Mr. Ryan busy, so I was thankful for it and looked deeper into the forge.

He was standing by the great anvil with a pile of miners' picks beside him. He held one in a big pair of tongs and was bringing his hammer down in a strong and steady rhythm onto the red-hot metal.

He glanced up and caught me watching him. He smiled, and I felt the heat from the fires so intolerable that my face burned, and I had to hasten away.

Mother was resting on the bed. Her brow was feverish and her face pale, but she was pleased to accept the mixture I had brought, and took some from a spoon for me.

"Not unpalatable," she murmured. "Tastes almost as though some spirituous liquor had gone into it. But of course that could not be so, could it, Ann?"

I assured her that it could not; I told her that Mr. Sly had seemed to be a stern and upright man, a strict teetotaler if I ever saw one, but privately I prayed that he had strongly fortified the medicine with spirits. Poor Mother needed all the help she could get. She smiled and drifted off to sleep.

I had some mending to do, so I took it outside to the bench that stands beneath the great gum tree that shelters our hut. It was pleasant to lift my eyes from my stitches every now and then to watch the water trickling by in the creek, but my peace was marred, as it was every day, by the noise of the men shouting, the stones rattling, and the heavy rake creaking as the poor horse plodded around and around in circles at the puddling machine close by.

Drays laden with clay and white pebbles of quartz came groaning to the machine, their contents were tipped out into a round trough, and water and the heavy rake device to which the patient horse was attached separated the clay from the gold. Young lads, sons of miners, were employed to pick out the gold-bearing quartz pebbles by hand, leaving a great pile of useless stone they called mullock beside the trough. I wished they would do it elsewhere; there had been no mullock heaps in Bloomsbury.

I was longing for the courage to chide them for their coarse language and looked up in the hope that the severity of my glance might quiet them.

And there he was, striding down the slope toward me! The young man from the smithy, with a bunch of pickaxes across his shoulders. Hurriedly I gathered up my mending and in my haste dropped my needle. I dared not leave it there in the dirt; needles, pins, and thimbles are scarce here and expensive to buy, so I was forced to flurry about on the ground beneath the bench in search of it. I found it at last and stood, only to find that the young man had not approached our hut after all but had gone instead to the puddling machine and was chatting intently to the men. Together they examined one of the pickaxes. He gave it to a miner, who, judging by the signs I was able to read, was unable to pay in cash and offered to settle his debt when he struck it rich on his claim.

They all laughed heartily at the man's antics, and I sat down again. The young man had not come to seek me, that was quite clear, and it certainly was not my intention to flee like a frightened deer simply because a fellow in whom I was not to the slightest degree interested might come near me.

But he was looking in my direction, and he caught me looking in his! I was mortified by my blushes and thereafter kept my head down and my eyes on my stitches— most of the time. He was wearing a gray flannel shirt and moleskin trousers that were none too clean, and heavy, dusty boots. He was clean shaven, and his thick black hair was long and curling on his neck. It was not possible for me to see the color of his eyes, peering as I was from such a difficult angle, but his form was very pleasing.

The rough cotton of the shirt I was mending felt like the finest silk as I sewed and felt the presence of the young man so near. But in truth he was showing little interest in me, and I knew that my parents would never consider him a suitable acquaintance. They had told me often enough that as soon as my father made his fortune in the goldfields, we would be returning to England and I would come out in society as a young lady of my station should.

But while I knew a triumphant return to England to be their fervent dream, I was quite unable to believe that it would ever come about. My father was spending altogether too much time at the bar of the Royal Hotel, talking about his hopes, and too little time digging his claim. I was not as confident as they that we should return to Bloomsbury as wealthy colonials.

I kept my head down as footsteps came nearer. They stopped beside my bench, and two pickaxes thudded to the ground.

I looked up. His eyes were as blue as mine were brown. A deep, velvet blue, and they were smiling at me.

"Excuse me, ma'am, would you be wanting to buy yourself an axe or two now?"

He was being insolent. Teasing me, and I had no idea of what to say to him.

Just then my mother's voice floated out from the win-

dow of the hut. "Do come inside now, Ann Bird," she
called. "I need your help. At once."

So that was that. I carefully replaced the needle in my
housewife before I stood up this time, and gave the
cheeky youth a cold glance as I passed.

He leaned on his pickaxes and touched his forehead
in salute. "Beautiful," he murmured, and as I turned,
he added, "the name. Ann Bird. A proper little melody
it is." And in his lilting voice it did sound like a song.

Then he picked up his implements and walked away,
and I entered the hut to face my mother's wrath.

"How dare you speak to that fellow, Ann Bird!" she
ranted in quite a strong voice considering how ill she had
been that very morning. "A common laborer. And filthy
as well."

I had a difficult decision to make, whether to remain
silent (knowing that my silences invariably drove my poor
mother to distraction) or to speak up (knowing that our
disputes invariably sent her sighing to her bed). I decided
to speak, but to be very wary of what I said.

"Yes, Mama, he was not very clean, was he? A lad
from the blacksmith's forge, so I suppose that explains
his grime."

"What did you speak about, child?"

"*I* did not speak at all, Mama."

"Well then, Miss Impudence, what did *he* say to *you*?"

Miss Impudence and Miss Importance, both in the
space of one day!

"Nothing of the slightest significance, Mama."

"Pray allow me to be the judge of that, miss. What
did he say to you?"

I could see that I had driven her far enough, so I smiled
at her in what I hoped was a disarming fashion. "He
asked if we had need of any pickaxes, Mama."

Despite her doubts and disapproval my mother had a

ready sense of humor, and she smiled back at me and asked for another draft of her elixir. I fetched it for her, then busied myself preparing the evening meal against the time when my father would return from his claim.

Our hut was spacious compared to some. My father had been fortunate in securing it from a disgruntled miner who was returning to Sydney. It was made of planks rough hewn from gum trees, and the walls were lined with canvas. The roof was of bark and the floor of earth, and the rafters were home to so many skittering, sly creatures that I seldom looked up for dread of nightmares. The central room served as our kitchen and drawing room, with a big, open fireplace, a rough table, and some chairs. Rooms opened on either side of this, bedrooms for my parents and myself. There was no glass for windows, but slab shutters opened upward to let in light and air. It was a snug little house, but a far cry from our dwelling in London.

But today I was disinclined to mourn our drastic change of circumstances and cheerfully set about my chores. First I fetched wood to liven up the fire, then filled a dipper from the water cask. The level in the cask was alarmingly low; I calculated that only with extreme care would we manage until the next visit of the water man. I looked forward to his visits; he was a cheerful old fellow with the longest beard I have seen, and he sang as he drove his heavy cart with the big barrel mounted on its frame between the wheels. He used rawhide buckets to fill the barrel with water from the spring three miles away, and by the time he had reached our settlement, he was ready for a rest, so he trusted me to hold the leather hose and fill our cask myself while he smoked his pipe and took his ease beneath our gum tree.

The nearby creek was useful in an emergency only, its water so foul and unclear as to be impossible to drink at all, and I had to leave it for hours for the mud to settle before using it for our washing. Father sometimes donned the wooden yoke that some Chinaman had left, and fetched water from it with a bucket hanging from each side of his shoulders, but his detestation of this menial task was so deep that I asked it of him only when we were in dire need.

Today as I gazed into the clear water of the cask, I saw velvet eyes smiling back at me. I quickly set the lid in place and took the dipper inside to fill the kettle. When it was swinging safely on its iron bar above the flames, I went to the meat cask and fetched a slab of mutton to boil for our dinner. I hummed a random tune as I worked, and this was sufficiently unusual to cause my mother to call from her bed.

"You sound very cheerful, my dear. How pleasant it is to hear you singing. Do you recall the harp that stood in the drawing room at home?"

Indeed I did, and I remembered my mother playing the harp and my father standing beside her, singing as she played. That thought took my happy mood away, and I went about the rest of my preparations in silence, uneasily awaiting the return of my father, who was far removed these days from the elegant, good-natured gentleman he had been back home in England.

Sally

I lay in the bathtub up to my ears in jasmine-scented bubbles and watched, speechless, while Annie examined the rip in my jeans, then turned her attention to the front, where the button had popped off and where the stone or whatever it was lay hidden in the pocket. I moaned in annoyance that she was about to find it—the very best thing I could have done actually, as she immediately dropped the pants and came across to see what the matter was. By her anxious expression I knew she thought I was about to drown, and I took my cue from that.

"Just a tiny twinge," I smiled bravely. "Would you put those awful jeans straight into the laundry basket please, Annie. I may be able to mend them, after they're washed of course. I really don't even want to see them now. They were brand new. Dad gave me the money just last week." I tried for a slight sob in my voice. "Please put them out of sight. Please?"

Good old Annie obliged, and after making quite sure that I'd be all right if left alone, she pottered off to the kitchen to prepare hot milk for me.

It would have been more convenient had she brought

in my night gear, but she didn't, so I eased myself out of the bath and gingerly patted my aching limbs into dryness, then I fished in the laundry basket and took my find from the pocket of the jeans. It did seem to be a lump of dried mud, but there *was* a gleam, so I sloshed it about in the bathwater for a while. At last the mud fell away. I sloshed it some more, then dried it carefully on the end of my towel.

It was a nugget of pure gold! Dull, scratched, and grimy, but just like the nuggets I'd seen at the museum. And set in the center of it was a small diamond.

I turned it over. On the back was a tiny hinge where a pin had made it into a brooch. There were also some words engraved there, but the letters were so tiny that I couldn't make them out.

"You okay, Sal? Your milk's ready. Want a hand? Leave the bath, I'll clean up for you."

"No, I'm right. Yes. Coming. Thanks, Annie," I blithered. Then I tucked the towel around me and trailed off to my bedroom with my treasure trove concealed in my hand.

I slipped it under the pillow intending to have a closer look at it when Annie could be persuaded to give up her vigil and go to bed herself, but I must have been more tired than I'd thought, because when I awoke it was morning.

She was still there, or there again, and now Aunt Bess was with her. They were both staring so intently at me that it was no wonder I'd woken up. Those four big dark eyes boring into one defenseless skull transmitted a lot of force, I can tell you.

Aunt Bess slapped a cold hand on my forehead and grabbed my wrist with the other cold hand.

"Well, that's a relief. No temp and her pulse seems steady enough. How do you feel, dear?"

Before I could answer, she was off again. "You should

have called us, Annie. Really! Only at the Comptons, could have been home in half an hour. Or Dr. Chan."

"I'm perfectly all—"

"He'll come at any time, you know that. He should have been called."

"But I don't need a—"

"Goodness me, what's Stella going to say when she hears her only child has fallen down a mine shaft! And in my care too."

I sat up quickly. If there was one thing my mother didn't need at the moment it was the news that this only child had fallen down a mine shaft. I'd been frantic to get away from her and Dad for a while, and I certainly didn't want either or both of them racing up to drag me back to safety, and to their quarrels and problems.

I shouted—it's the only way to get Aunt Bess's attention. I thought the whole family was incredibly rude to her when I first arrived two days ago, but now I shouted as loudly as any of them. Except Uncle James, who didn't even wait for her to start talking before *he* bawled.

"Look! See! I'm okay! Really I am, Aunt Bess." Then I tossed my legs out of the bed, which was quite heroic of me really because I did feel more like snuggling down for a while longer.

"I think she's all right, Mum, really. Nothing seems broken, she's just got a few little cuts and bruises. None of the cuts was even bleeding last night when she'd had a bath."

We all had our own reasons for playing down my injuries. Annie didn't fancy being accused by her mother of neglecting me. Aunt Bess didn't fancy being accused by her best friend, *my* mother, of the same thing. And I didn't want my parents to take me home. So we were all satisfied when Aunt Bess gently pushed me back onto the pillows and tucked the duvet around my chin.

"All right, then. You snuggle down for a while longer,

dear. It's a bit nippy this morning. We'll see about letting your parents know later on. Annie will bring you up some breakfast, and when you've had that, I want you to try to go to sleep again. Nothing like a good sleep to make you feel better, and if there's anything at all you want, dear, just you shout. Don't hesitate. Annie will fetch it for you. Anything at all you fancy."

They went out the door, Aunt Bess still chattering and Annie giving me a baleful glare, thinking no doubt of the busy day I could give her if I wanted to. I did want to, but as it happened I slept most of the time and didn't feel up to planning things for her to fetch for me. She quite cheerfully brought in trays of food and offered to sit with me. I didn't accept the offer, I was afraid the argument we'd begun the night before might start up again, and I needed to be in better shape for that than I was at the moment.

David came in with her when she brought my lunch, and stared at me from the foot of the bed as if he imagined I was at my last gasp or something. He didn't say a word and looked so worried that I finally put him out of his misery by assuring him that I was quite well, only sleepy, and that his rescue of the previous night had been appreciated. He grinned then and gave me an almost cheerful wave as he went out.

After dinner there was a timid knock and Cooper put his head around the door. "All right if I come in for a minute?"

I had no makeup on and no doubt my hair looked less than glamorous, but he came in anyway and sat on the foot of the bed. Cooper is twenty and doesn't bother much with girls. Well, he certainly hadn't been bothering much with me, and Annie he just treats like a kid sister, which she is, so fair enough. He looked uncomfortable and I guessed that Aunt Bess had sent him, or nagged him into coming.

"Look, I'm sorry about last night. . . ." he started.

"It's all right. I'm hardly bruised at all."

"No, I didn't mean that. . . ."

"Oh, you mean the discussion we were having?" Some discussion. An all-in brawl, more like.

"Listen. Will you just shut up and listen to me for one minute? I mean I'm sorry we laughed at you, down the mine shaft. And joked about hauling you up."

"That's all right, Cooper," I said, and was prepared to be forgiving until he went on.

"I guess we were all so fed up with you really. You do go on with a lot of rubbish, you know."

"Oh, great. Thanks."

"And it's not as if you even know what you're talking about. I mean, what would you know about farmers and their problems?"

"My father does. He knows about everyone's problems; he's an accountant, for goodness' sake. If anyone knows, he does, and he says farmers are always complaining about being poor, yet they send their children to boarding school and drive around in Mercedes and Volvos and stuff."

"I told you, the distances we cover, the roads up here, a farmer needs a good reliable car—"

"He says most farmers are just inefficient, *that's* why they're—"

He stood up. "Yes, I know what your *father* thinks, Sally. You told us last night. I'd better go now. Mum said I wasn't to upset you. Sorry. Good night. Hope you feel better in the morning."

He walked out, and I felt cheated. He'd managed once more to treat me like a stupid child. Or like a hysterical teenager, which was obviously how he saw me. I also felt cheap, because it wasn't fair of me to trot out my father's prejudices and use them in place of my own opinions. Worst of all, I felt ashamed, because he was right, and I really didn't know what I was talking about.

I hated Cooper for making me feel that way.

It was my first visit to the farm, and I really had wanted to enjoy it. I'd known the Coopers all my life. Annie is a boarder at the school I go to, and Aunt Bess and Uncle James stay with us each Easter when they come down for the Royal. But my father always says Aunt Bess is boring and talks too much, so we'd never stayed with them.

Now, of course, things were changing. Dad's criticisms of Aunt Bess were nothing to the criticisms he was now making of Mom. She was doing her bit too, of course. They seemed to bicker about every tiny thing, when they were speaking to each other, that is. For most of the time the house was foggy with their silences. I could just tolerate the arguments and could even cope with the silences, but what really got to me was the way each gave me messages to transmit to the other. *That* really soured me, and finally I did something about it.

It was Saturday afternoon, Dad's usual golf day, but this time he stayed at home and got out the lawn mower.

"Thought you'd be going to your golf," Mom remarked, in a quite normal tone of voice I thought.

"Well, as you can see, I am not going to *my* golf." His voice was tight with anger. "You *said* the lawn needed mowing, therefore I am missing my golf and mowing the lawn for you. Are you satisfied?"

"No, I am not satisfied." Mother's voice was at the same deadly quiet pitch as his now. "You are not mowing the lawn for me. You are mowing the lawn because *you* want to mow the lawn, or because you do not wish to play golf today. You are not mowing the lawn for *me*!"

"Very well, Stella. I refuse to discuss it any further with you. Sally, tell your mother that I am mowing this lawn in an endeavour to keep the outside of this house neat, however much the inside may be neglected."

Well, I didn't fancy relaying *that* message to Ma. She'd heard it anyway and was marching purposefully toward the door. I knew what she planned to do. It was what she always did when she and Pa had this kind of argument. She'd drag all the furniture into the middle of all the rooms and vacuum all the floors that she couldn't scrub and polish. The rest she'd scrub and polish. *Then* she'd wash every article of clothing that we weren't actually wearing at the time, *then* she'd iron like a maniac for the rest of the day and most of the night. And if I offered to help, she'd snap my head off and tell me to read a book or something, enjoy myself while I was still young and free. Young and free! So help me, at times like that I felt older than both of them put together, and with about as much freedom as the prisoner of Zenda, whoever *he* was.

On this particular Saturday afternoon I had had enough. I wasn't the one quarreling, so I could see no reason why I should be dragged into it.

"I will not!" I shouted, much louder than I had meant to. "I'm not going to. Any more. And I wish you'd stop . . . scrubbing, and . . . mowing, and . . . ironing . . . and, and polishing that lawn!" To my horror I was bawling my head off as I were a little kid, and I just couldn't stop!

I must have been raising quite a storm, because Dad stopped the mower in mid-mow and Mum rushed across and grabbed me and hauled me inside and sat me down and patted my arm, and then Dad actually poured me a brandy! If I'd only known that losing my temper could lead to being offered hard liquor I would certainly have done it sooner. And often.

I went to bed early that night and heard them talking until very late. But it was quiet talking, and in the morning Mum made a telephone call to Aunt Bess. The result was that as soon as the school holidays began, which fortunately was soon, I was on the train for Gulgong and two weeks' holiday at Uncle James's property.

Thinking about it all made me quite weepy, completing the job that my conversation with Cooper had begun. So I took my secret nugget from beneath the pillow and looked at it again. I still couldn't decipher what was written on the back, but it was a comfort to feel its rough surface, and I polished it for while on the sheet.

Before I went to sleep, I reasoned that Uncle James would no doubt own a magnifying glass, and neither he nor Aunt Bess were likely to ask questions if I wanted to borrow it.

So I had something interesting to do tomorrow and would keep out of Cooper's way as much as possible.

Ann

IF I were to offer my mother one piece of advice, it would be this: Do not ask Papa how things went at the mine the moment he walks in the door of the hut! She does it every day, and every day his answer is a trifle more cool and short. *I* know how things are going without having to ask. They are going from bad to hopeless, and any day now he is going to give up in despair. Heaven only knows what we shall do then!

My father is a gentleman, handsome, educated and of obvious refinement, but unfortunately none of these attributes serves him well here. There are few gentlemen of his rank or presence on the goldfields, or if they are here, they conceal their backgrounds very carefully. We brought no books with us from England, apart from Mother's Bible, and there is of course no lending library at the diggings, so we are all deprived of reading. As for his refinement, it only serves to make him feel apart from the other miners, so that we have very little company and no friends at all.

So when I saw the notice nailed to the post by the baker's shop, I supposed it would be of no interest to our family at all.

GRAND GYMKHANA AND SOCIAL
EASTER SATURDAY
INQUIRE WITHIN

But I hastened home to tell my mother just in case.

That evening when Father came home, she asked him the usual question about his day at the mine and received the usual answer.

"I had no luck today, Mary. Although someone quite nearby bottomed on gold—I saw the red flag raised and wished them well. But I had no luck. My mine is a duffer."

The trouble with my father is that he gives in too easily to despair. He would take no advice from those already here and chose the site of his digging, I consider, merely for its convenience. It is not far from our hut and within easy walking of the township. Others are prepared to go farther afield and toil for longer hours, but not my father.

This evening, however, he surprised me. He actually mentioned the gymkhana himself and suggested that we might all attend! The fact that it was to be held on the property of the local "squire" may have had some bearing on his decision.

"I think we should all support these community functions," he said grandly. "It may amuse you, Mary, and give Ann some opportunity of meeting the young people of the district."

There was only one young person of the district that I cared to meet, but I kept my mouth tightly closed as I cleared away the dishes, partly to stop myself from uttering a word that might change Father's mind and partly to conceal my glee. I knew *he* would be there. He *looked* as if gymkhanas would be just his style!

Easter came, and Mother was pleased, because a minister of religion had come to the district and a service was to be held on Good Friday. There is no church here, so the service took place in the home of the local butcher, Mr. Dobson, a very pious man. We arrived too late to obtain a seat inside the shack, but Mother was satisfied to listen from outside the door, and afterward the clergyman came and spoke to us. I found little comfort in his words myself, and he was too obviously in a great hurry to climb into his carriage and move on to his next appointment—a hearty dinner, I fancy, at the big house over the hill.

It was gusty with mizzles of rain on Good Friday, but Saturday dawned fine, and we dressed carefully. I wore my best plaid dress, and Mother lent me her cable stitch shawl. Father would not promise that we could attend the social that evening but said he would consider that when he saw how the day went.

I fervently hoped that it would go well for him!

When we arrived, the day's festivities had already begun. Families were parading in their best dress, with the children tumbling about begging their parents for pennies to buy ginger beer. There were contests for the men— running, hammer throwing, woodchopping—and events for the ladies such as nail driving and rolling-pin throwing. The children were catered for with footraces and lolly scrambles.

The tiny person who had objected to being referred to as my father's "good woman" was there with her husband and all their children, cheering them on with her stentorian voice in every contest. Of course, we took no part in any of these, although I swear I could have driven nails faster and thrown my rolling pin farther than any woman there had I been given the chance! But in order to be permitted to stay for the social, I was willing to bow to my father's wishes all day and be very demure and refined.

There were benches set up beneath the trees, and

Mother was happy to sit there and watch. As I walked away, I turned to wave to her and was both pleased and saddened by the picture I saw. Behind her was the imposing homestead and its well-tended garden, so much more fitting a background for her than the rough hut we lived in. She was in every way suited to be the mistress of this grand property, and I know she would have enjoyed the comforts it would offer.

As I looked at her the front door of the house opened and a young man came out on to the veranda. There was something familiar about him, and as he walked down the steps and along the path toward us, I remembered where I had seen him before. He was the other customer in Mr. Sly's pharmacy when I had purchased the physic for Mother's chill.

He came through the gate and walked directly toward where my mother was seated, so I returned to her side in case she needed me. Of course, I had no desire to meet the young man, but Mother is shy and very mindful of the proprieties. He paused beside us and bowed to Mama.

"I trust you are comfortable, ma'am," he said, then turned to me, bowed again, and quickly moved away before either of us could answer.

Mother was delighted to be noticed, and commented on what a handsome young man he was. I was less impressed. He had asked a question and had not waited for a reply. I wondered what he would have done had I said, "Indeed, sir, we are not comfortable at all. Would you kindly do something about it?"

The thought made me giggle, and fortunately Mama thought I was smiling with joy at having been noticed by the son of the big landowner! I did not think him very handsome. He was tall and thin, with fair hair and brown eyes, but I prefer darker hair and blue eyes myself.

There were many stalls set under the trees, offering a variety of refreshments, so I went to fetch a cool drink for us both. And serving at the drinks stall was the young man from the forge! I failed to notice him until I was right at the counter ready to give my order. There was no way of escaping, as the crowd was pressing upon me from behind.

"And what can I get for you, Miss Ann Bird?" He smiled, and I quickly checked the list chalked on the board behind him.

"I should like a glass of . . . gingerette for my mother, and . . . a glass of . . . shrub for myself, if you please."

His laughter affected most of the crowd, and they guffawed most rudely around me. When he was able to control his mirth, he said, "A shrub for yourself? Are you sure now?"

"I am sure," I told him very firmly.

"You take a glass of shrub now and then, do you?"

"I drink it regularly." I wondered how firm I had to be with this rude man.

Then a woman beside me spoke up. Beside me and below me. I recognized her as my tiny friend with the grievance and the seven children.

"You won't be wanting shrub, dearie," she advised. " 'Tis a brew of rum and orange juice, with a pinch of spice in it. Not a drink for a young lady like yourself."

He waited, still grinning.

"Kindly serve me with two glasses of gingerette." I was furious with him for being so odious to me. But as he put the glasses on the counter, he looked straight into my eyes and whispered, "Sorry. 'Twas a joke! Could you not give us a smile then, Ann Bird?"

And in spite of my annoyance, I could not help but smile back at him, and then I laughed, and so did all the crowd, and I hurried away with my beverages in case my father heard the mirth and came to see what it was about, and chided me for associating with my inferiors. If Father ever came home and caught me chatting with the water man and allowing him to take his ease while I filled our barrel myself, I think he would order the old man never to return, and be happy to allow us all to die of thirst rather than to have me talk to him on such familiar terms! Poor Father. It must be a sore trial to him to have such a daughter, but I do try, most of the time, to behave as he and Mama wish. The trouble is, I find it more difficult to be dutiful as each day passes.

As I made my way back to where Mama was waiting, the young man from the homestead came up to me. He smiled again, but in a very lukewarm way. No jokes from this one!

"Excuse me, Miss. I wondered . . . My name is Charles. I wondered . . ."

I wondered too why he was diffident and stammering, so to ease his misery, I said, "My name is Ann. Is there some way I can help you, sir?"

"Well . . . yes . . . I wondered . . . if you plan to attend the social this evening . . . the . . . dance . . . to be held there, in my father's woolshed." And he pointed to the imposing shed beyond the house. It was fashioned of stone, like the homestead itself, and was twenty times bigger than the tiny abode we lived in. But I could not blame him for that.

"I think not," I replied calmly. I was about to add that my father would make that decision and he had not yet told us of his plans, but the young man did not wait for me to elaborate, but nodded as if he had received the answer he expected, and hurried away. He *was* a queer one, I thought as I set off through the crowd to find Mama.

A pleasant surprise awaited me. My father was there

beside my mother, and he had decided that we should attend the dance after all! I pretended great calm at the decision but had to take care that my seeming lack of enthusiasm did not make him change his mind. I had never been to a social in my life, and the very thought of it set my toes to dancing. I wondered who else would be there, if anyone I knew might ask me to dance! And if my father would permit it, if he did.

I drank my gingerette and it tasted, I swear, like the best and costliest champagne!

We arrived in good time for the social. Mother and I had bustled about to prepare a plate of sandwiches to bring for supper. A trestle table was set along one wall of the shed, and a great feast of cold meats, sandwiches, and cakes was displayed. In a small room to one side several small children and babies lay sleeping on the floor, and in the middle of the shed two men were engaged in a peculiar rite. Each held a wax candle and a knife, and as they moved across the floor, they whittled at the candles and spread the wax at their feet.

"Makes it easier for dancing," my father explained. "But I fear it will take more than candle wax to make this floor conform to London standards."

"We are not in London now, Papa," I whispered. "No doubt it will do quite well. Will you dance with me?" He looked at me sharply, sensing a rebuke, then recovered his composure and conducted Mama and me to seats along the wall.

He led my mother out for the first dance, but the condition of the floor did not suit him, and when they returned to their places, he was quite out of sorts.

"We shall not stay long," he said. "This is not at all the sort of entertainment I had expected. You may watch the dancing for a time, and I shall return for you later."

Then he set off toward the door, leaving Mama and me alone. I was angry that I had not had my dance with him, and Mama was sympathetic.

"It's not at all like home, dear," she murmured. "But should you wish to join in the fun, you have my permission. Unless, of course, your father returns and forbids it."

I sometimes wonder why my mother takes such heed of my father's moods and importances. She is a kindly woman and one to enjoy life, yet she allows his decisions to sway us all. I decided at that very moment that should I ever marry, I would stand *beside* my husband, not in his shadow.

In this mood I found it difficult to settle to the evening's entertainment, but soon the music had me tapping my foot, and hoping that someone, anyone, would ask me to dance. No one did.

Charles, who had been so indecisive that afternoon at the gymkhana, came to stand by the wall opposite us. He gazed at me for some time, wondering no doubt at seeing me there when I had been so definite that we should not be attending. I smiled but received only a stiff nod in return before he joined a group of young people and invited one of them to dance. I kept the smile on, although a certain stiffness developed after a time. I was determined that I should appear to be enjoying myself.

The music was provided by a concertina, two violins, and a piano (kindly lent, I heard someone say, by the squatter's wife), all played with great gusto but little skill. The effect, however, was very bright and bouncy, and I longed to be on the floor dancing with the rest of them.

There was no sign of the dark-haired young man from the forge. Not that I was seeking him at all, but his was a face that I knew, and I had expected to see him there.

I kept a close watch on the doorway, not for him, of course, but in case my father might return and ask me to dance. He did not.

Suddenly there was a small commotion by the door, and in came the person himself to break into the circle with a very pretty girl whom I had seen once or twice before. Her mother ran the Empire Boarding House and Dining Rooms, and her figure was very fine. The daughter's, I mean; the mother was monstrously fat, and I wondered if in time even the daughter would run to plumpness if she was not careful. I checked her ankles as she galloped past me—they *were* inclined to thickness, poor girl.

After that dance was over, Papa came back to stand by the door. I was almost hoping that he had come to take us home, as there was little enjoyment to be had here and surely Mother was becoming weary.

I was about to ask if she would like to go when the master of ceremonies announced the next dance. A mazurka. I fixed my smile on again and looked completely disinterested, so that no one should think that *I* wished to be invited on to the floor.

"Would you fancy a dance with me, then?" The dark young man was standing in front of us. I began to stand up and turned to my mother. She, seeing my father across the room, quietly but definitely said, "No, thank you, sir. My daughter is not available to dance with you."

I sat down again, my smile almost tearing my face apart. He nodded, unsmiling, and walked quickly away.

From the other side of the room Charles approached. I think he had not seen the other's invitation and my mother's refusal, because he came right up and addressed her.

"Good evening, Ma'am. Would you permit me to dance with your daughter?"

From his position at the doorway my father beamed. Mother, of course, said yes, and we walked out onto the floor.

I had been longing to join in all evening, yet now I felt only sullenness and anger. Charles might be the squatter's son, but to me he was nought but a tedious bore.

Sally

THE aroma of bacon frying and bread toasting
while you are lolling in bed is one of life's sweet
pleasures, and I was enjoying this quietly the next morning when Annie came crashing into my room with my
breakfast tray.

"No doubt about it, Sally, you are a lucky beggar,
falling down that mine!"

I failed to see the justice in that remark and told her
so, meanwhile grabbing the tray and setting its little legs
in place a split second before all its contents went over-
board onto my duvet.

"Well, you must admit it is unfair. Mom says you're
to have at least another day in bed, more if you want it,
and here I am doing all the work. I did think that when
you came, you might give me a hand around the place."
She sat down and began buttering a piece of my toast.
For herself, of course. Stole a slice of my bacon, too, to
go with it, so I had to eat really fast. But I managed to
comment between mouthfuls that if she thought bringing
a few trays of food to a friend suffering intense pain too
difficult to manage then she was hardly the stuff that
friends are made of. "But don't worry about me," I
told her.

"I'm not," she stated quite definitely.

. . . I was willing to get up straight away, if that was what she wanted, look after myself, take the burden off her hands . . .

"Great," she said, "hurry up then, you can help me feed the horses."

That was not exactly what I had in mind, but she bustled out before I could qualify my offer. I was feeling perfectly well, in fact. Aunt Bessie had painted my scratches lavishly with gentian violet, so with that and a few bruises I glowed in glorious Technicolor, but my stiffness had gone and there was no pain, so I could hardly loaf around any longer. But I should have inquired first just what "feeding the horses" entailed!

I chose the likeliest-looking pair of rubber boots from the row that marched along the back veranda. Miles too big they were; the boots moved quite independently of my feet, which slipped forward and backward with each step I took.

It had rained a bit during the night. Not enough to make the slightest difference to the empty dams, but enough to make me slither and slide as I stumped down the track after Annie. I noticed that she had her jeans tucked inside her boots, so I paused at the cattle ramp and tucked mine in too. She didn't wait for me, of course, but plodded on toward the sheds and the yards where the horses were waiting.

She dragged the heavy metal door open, and we stepped into the shed. Talk about untidy! I've never seen such clutter. An old red tractor thing stood in the middle, the floor was dirt, saddles and bridles and all that junk they use on horses hung from the posts, and big bags of what I supposed was feed were stacked everywhere. Along one wall was a row of bins with a pile of buckets at one end, and the whole place smelled suffocatingly of chaff, wheat, oats, and of course manure.

"Now, here's what we do," Annie directed me as she lifted the lids off the bins. "Each bin has a scoop in it, see? There's a bucket for each horse, and this is what they get. Blackie gets one of this, two of this, one of this, and a handful only of this, and none of that, right? Ugly gets *two* of this, one of this, one of this, and none of that, right? Sam gets one of this, two of this, one of—"

"Annie," I murmured weakly, "why don't you ladle out the stuff, and I'll carry it to the horses. I'll never remember."

"Okay," she said, "right." And I realized from the brisk tone of her voice that I'd walked into a trap. There was no doubt about it—Annie on the farm was a different girl from the Annie I knew at school. A lot more sneaky.

She filled the buckets for Blackie and Ugly. "Out that door and they're the two farthest away."

I took a bucket in each hand, nudged the back door open with my elbow, stepped outside, and almost expired on the spot with fright.

The light shower of rain that had turned the track from the house into a slippery slide had really made a mess in the horse paddocks. I was walking in thick chocolate fudge along a narrow path, and over the fence on each side of me was a row of snorting, tossing horses' heads, with the rest of the horses attached, of course, all desperately and viciously trying to grab me as I skated by. Someone should invent something better than boots to tackle mud, although if mine had been a snugger fit, I might have managed with more dignity.

I made it to the far gate without being eaten alive and put one of the buckets down so that I could slip the catch open. Immediately a monster nose came through the lower space of the fence straight into the bucket, and with great snufflings and grunts of delight one of the horses had a breakfast he wasn't entitled to. I watched forlornly as he finished it off, clutching the other bucket to my bosom to keep it safe from other predatory beasts. And I realized that I'd forgotten which bucket belonged to which horse! Had this animal, a complete stranger to me, helped himself to the meal carefully measured for Blackie? Or was poor old Ugly the loser this time?

I left the now-empty bucket where it lay on its side in the mud and opened the gate. And stepped into the worst quagmire the world has ever seen! The horses' hooves had churned it up to such an extent that there was hardly a space big enough to accommodate a human-sized foot in the entire yard. I lurched from hollow to crest of soft mud, slid in mounds of manure, and fended off the slavering faces of two enormous, champing horses. There was a feed tin in the far corner of the yard, and I finally reached it, still cuddling my bucket with both hands.

"Now which of you is . . . er, Ugly?" I inquired pleasantly enough, although from that angle they both looked extremely ugly to me. Neither gave the slightest sign of recognizing his name, so I emptied the bucket into the tin and let them take potluck, then sidled carefully past, giving wide berth to their hindquarters, as Annie had warned me to do, and shut the gate. I picked up the empty bucket on the way and reported back to my superior that Blackie and Ugly had been taken care of.

"Gave them the right ones, did you?"

"Oh, sure. Why? Does it matter?"

"You bet it does. No oats for Ugly."

"Right. No oats for Ugly." I didn't dare ask why, just in case a meal containing oats was certain to send Ugly into a screaming conniption involving homicidal mania or something. In any case he was only getting half rations this morning, so it shouldn't affect him too badly.

I took the next two buckets, was directed to the last

gate on the right, and told these were both the same menus. It was from the last yard on the right that the marauding beast had stuck his head and stolen the bucket of food, but I was in no mood to point the finger of accusation at anyone, so I let myself through the gate and flung the two buckets into the waiting tins. The earlier snack hadn't spoiled his appetite, whichever one it was, because they both tucked in immediately and were nuzzling greedily at my neck as I lurched through the morass back to the shed.

"How's it going?" Kind of her to ask.

"Great." I said. "Great. Loving it."

"Horses are beautiful creatures, aren't they?"

Not this lot, I thought. Greedy, grasping, rude, pushy crowd of steaming brutes, these are. "Yes," I cooed, "beautiful."

This time I had to make sure that the gray got the bucket in my right hand, the chestnut the one in my left. That was not, however, what the horses wanted. As soon as I was through the gate, I felt the bucket in my right hand suddenly grow a lot heavier. I looked down, and there was a huge chestnut face buried deep in the feed, and the level was being lowered at an alarming rate. I yanked at the bucket and managed to spill half the contents of the other one in the process while making no impression on the hungry horse on my right.

"Hey, you!" I bellowed. "Get your great, greedy face out of there!" He refused and kept on chomping at the forbidden food. "To hell with the lot of you then! Take it all! Eat the lot!" I shouted "And I hope it chokes you!"

I stamped a foot in fury, and my stupid outsize boot squelched in the mud, and over I went, showering myself with the contents of the second bucket and landing in a steaming pile of mud and muck. The gray horse leaned down and proceeded to snuffle up the scattered feed from on and around my person. I was too furious to cry, and too terrified to move.

Annie strolled out as I lay there, and after she'd finished laughing, she shooed the gray away, helped me to my feet, and carried the buckets back to the shed.

"You sit there, I'll finish them off."

I sat on an upturned bucket, couldn't bury my head in my hands, couldn't move, nor ever would again, every part of me was so *filthy* and *smelly* and *stiff*. So I stared forlornly at the farthest corner of the shed, and would you believe it, at that very moment a mouse chose to poke its head out of a space beside a box full of old bits of rusty car parts. Actually, I'm almost certain it was a rat. A big one. But I didn't stop to find out, I screamed and ran, clawed the big doors open and scrambled back up the path to the house. When I was at the top of the rise, I looked back and there was Annie, in one of the horse yards, looking up at me as if I'd come from Mars or somewhere.

"Don't forget the bulls!" she called. "They're next."

"Bulls? What bulls? Where bulls?" I gibbered, but she couldn't have heard me because she just waved a bucket at me and strolled back into the shed. Honestly, country people are *weird*.

As I tottered into the kitchen, Aunt Bess sniffed and without even turning around said, "Make it a quick shower, could you, dear. Water's a bit low. And leave your clothes by the back door. *Out*side."

So I did, and when I was clean again, I asked if she had a magnifying glass and might I borrow it to examine an odd leaf I'd found. Dear old Aunt Bess was too busy to pry, and she directed me to Uncle James's desk. I found the glass, battered and scarred, underneath a pile of bills and letters and scurried into my room with it. I took the nugget brooch from under my pillow and focused on its back.

The words came up clearly, set one beneath the other. They were roughly scratched, some letters out of proportion, but the message was:

ANN

BIRD

JEM

EVER

I wondered what it could possibly mean, but not for long, because Annie was pounding on my door and going on about the bulls again.

Believe me, the horses were nothing compared to the bulls!

Uncle James and the boys had been working at a big, noisy machine near the shearing sheds, preparing feed for the cattle. They were all wearing face masks to protect themselves from the fine dust that was flying all about them. Now they took off the masks and hefted great sacks of the stuff onto the back of the truck. Cooper was at the wheel, and it was our job, Annie's and mine, to deliver the rations to the bulls in the hill paddocks. Uncle James and David headed off in the opposite direction with the four-wheel drive, similarly laden.

I didn't mind leaping off to open the gates, and I didn't mind being jounced along over the rough ground so that my knees were permanently dislocated and my teeth irreversably loosened. What I did take exception to was the supposition by the other two that there was nothing scary about bulls!

These animals were *enormous*! They milled around the truck as we drew up, pawing the ground and snorting and glaring at me. We dragged a bag of feed off the bed of the truck, me still on board shoving while the others pulled; then I was supposed to lug it across to their feed bin with Annie while Cooper got the next one ready to go. You try it sometime with a couple of thousand tons of bull, wild of eye and foaming at the mouth, nudging you in the ribs to hustle along please, he's mighty hungry, and so are all his burly pals. And they're *breathing* on you. Fire and brimstone. I did it, of course, holding my breath in terror, and I swear those animals have never been fed so fast!

We had a group of bulls in each of three paddocks to do, and I did hope that my fear might abate a little with familiarity. It didn't. All the blood in my body had completely congealed, and I must have been blue in the face by the time I closed the last gate on the way back. The old truck juttered back to the sheds, and as we tottered off Cooper came around and slapped me on the shoulder.

"Thanks for the help, Sal," he murmured. "Weren't scared, were you?"

"Scared? Me? Of a few friendly little pets like that?"

He accepted that as a no answer, and even Annie came good with a grin and a wink. She knew, but in the worthy cause of feminist solidarity she wasn't going to tell.

During the enormous lunch that Aunt Bess served up, I asked nonchalantly if there was a family called Ever in the district.

"Not around here that I know of . . ."

"Why?"

"There are some Everetts closer to town—you know them, James . . ."

"What you want to know for?"

"Got it! You're thinking of old Mr. Evans, lives across the river . . ."

"Well, Bess, I've lived here all my life, and I don't recall any family called Everett . . ."

"Ever. It's Ever."

"Evans is close. Won't Evans do, Sal?"

"I'm sure it's Everett. Little bald man with lots of big teeth . . ."

"*What* do you want to know for?"

"Yes, dear, do you know these people?"

". . . *nor* any family called Ever. And Sally wouldn't know old Barney Evans, Davey. He's practically a recluse."

I'd opened a big enough can of worms, so I pretended that the name had just come to me, must have seen it in the local paper, or some name like it, or some name not even remotely resembling it, and it really didn't matter at all.

I had planned to ask next if they knew any family with the name of Bird, but decided not to bother.

So,

ANN

BIRD

JEM

EVER

remained a mystery to me. For the time being.

Ann

AFTER the miserable evening I had spent at the social, I wished to see no one, ever again, especially Charles. As a dancer he was a chuckleheaded ass, speaking not a word to me, but diligently counting the steps as we went, one-two-three, one-two-three, while watching every move of our feet as he did so. Later, when we waltzed together (no choice of mine I do assure you; I think my parents had forced him to ask me again by the strength of their gaze and the concentrated power of their prayers), above the counting came an agonized muttering every now and then, in the form of, "*I* am now *go*-hoing *to*-hoo reverse," and reverse we did, my poor feet suffering badly from the maneuver!

And all the while the boy from the forge glided and dipped and smiled at his partners without a care in the world. I know such exuberance is vulgar, but he did appear to be enjoying himself. And so did the girls he danced with.

After the waltz Father suggested we should leave. Mama was very tired and pale, so we left the music and the dancing and walked home, Father supporting Mother, and I guiding them both with the lantern. When we came to the ford I longed to take off my boots and ease my poor, mangled toes in the cool water, but Father had been imbibing strong drink at the woolshed, and I had to watch carefully lest he and Mother both topple from the stones.

We arrived home at last, and I fell into my bed, weary, sore, and angry.

A few days after that something happened that may influence to a very small degree my feelings for this place.

There is a band of Indian hawkers who travel about the country selling all manner of things to the miners and their wives. They come with bundles and baskets balanced on top of their heads, enormous loads some of them; the baker's wife (she of the small stature and large family) told me that once she had seen one with a cabin trunk teetering atop his turban! Whether I should believe her is another matter.

They sell calicoes and cottons, needles, pins, and thimbles, buttons and boots, and even pieces of exotic jewelry. Mother always glows when they come to our house; she dearly loves to swathe their colorful materials around her thin shoulders and deck herself with their silver and gold. But of course we have no money to buy such frivolous things, so we have to send them away.

On the day I am speaking of, the Afghans (as they were called) had finished their morning's trading and were gathered by the creek. I had walked to Mr. Chan Lee the Chinaman's garden to seek fresh vegetables, and I came upon them preparing their meal. The smell was delicious! All spices and curry and *flavor*! It was so different from our dreary old boiled mutton and damper that I paused to relish it for a moment.

Immediately there was pandemonium! The Indians jumped up and shouted at me, shooed me with their arms, and attempted to chase me away. Having done no wrong that I was aware of, I stood my ground and politely asked what was troubling them. My civility had no effect, however, and they shouted all the louder as I moved nearer with my queries.

Suddenly there was a whoop from behind me and the sound of running feet. My arm was clutched and I was twirled away from the Indians' reach by the black-haired young man from the forge!

"Don't mind her at all," he called to the angry men. "She means no harm, I assure you. Fool woman! Knows nothing! Nothing at all! No harm! Idiot woman! Idiot!"

While he was shouting he was pulling me away, and my basket of vegetables was in danger of spilling; but the Indians *did* appear to be pacified, so I decided to go with him, and say my piece and maybe box his ears later.

We ran together along the bank of the creek, and by the time we reached the ford the men had returned to their cooking. There is a stand of willows there, and a cool grassy bank beneath, so we paused to catch our breaths, to straighten my basket and its contents, and for me to vent my anger.

"How dare you speak of me like that!" I glared. "I was doing no harm at all. I am not foolish. I am not an idiot, and how dare you!"

He said nothing, just smiled his soft smile at me with his blue eyes staring straight into mine, and suddenly I stopped. We were both silent for a moment, then he said, "There now, that's better. Be calm. The Indians were bothered by your shadow, you see."

"I do not see. Why should my shadow bother some Indian hawkers? I did nothing to harm them. Nothing!"

"You didn't need to. They are of the Hindu religion, and if the shadow of a white person, an infidel, passes over their food, that food is contaminated. Now what do you think of that, Ann Bird?"

"I don't think very much of it, sir, and you are very free with my name. May I know yours?"

"You may. Jem Brady, at your service. Soon to be wealthy miner, I am, and hailing from the beautiful town of Kenmare. In Ireland, you know."

"I know," I snapped, although I truly did not. His voice was Irish, so I suppose I could have guessed eventually. "A miner? But I saw you working in the forge. Just happened to notice. As I passed by."

"I did indeed work in the forge, he said, "with old Ryan and his boys. But only till I could set up as a miner. Been working at every job I could get to save up money for the license and to live on until I strike it rich." He smiled mischievously. "Then I'll come courting you, Ann Bird."

I was mightily glad that neither of my parents was nearby to hear *that*!

"And now, be off home with you. That mama of yours would have a thousand fits if she saw you speaking to me. What a common person, to be asking her daughter to dance!"

I laughed. His voice was so charming. "A t'ousand fits!" A *million*, more like!

"I am sorry," I offered, embarrassed by my mother's timidity.

"Don't you worry." He smiled. "If I was your mother I'd never be letting you out of the house, I wouldn't." He took my hand in his. "My claim is on the side of the hill over yonder." He waved and I marked the place. "Will you walk this way again, Ann Bird? And will you think of me as a friend? For the time being, that is."

"Very well, Jem Brady. For the time being. A friend." I left him standing there beneath the willows, and I crossed the ford and took my vegetables home for our dinner, and all the way up the tiresome hill my feet scarce touched the ground. A friend! Of course, my parents would disapprove, and of course, I agreed with their sentiments. Entirely.

The Chinaman grew very wholesome vegetables, and I often had occasion to visit his farm. My mother was often weak and ill, and I did my best to build up her strength, but I confess that there was another reason for my journeys across the ford. Jem's mine was on the side of the far hill, and he worked hard and long at it. But when I had passed by humming a tune and had paused by the willows at the ford to recover my breath from the long and arduous walk, he would come and join me there, and we would sit on the bank under the willow tree's sweet curtaining fronds and talk for a while.

He told me of his home in Kenmare, "the greenest and brightest spot in all of Ireland," of the river running down to the sea and the mountains cragging up to Killarney's lakes—Macgillycuddy's Reeks, he called them. What a fine, imaginative name for a range of mountains! And Moll's Gap, where his grandfather lived, and the Gap of Dunloe, where the gypsies run their horses. He told me of the famine that had blighted his land and of the thousands who had starved and still were starving there.

I could listen to him forever and could feel in my heart the green and the warmth of the land that he had come from, and I could sense in my soul its sadness and oppression. Bloomsbury seemed a very pale place in comparison.

Our visits together were brief. Too many people moved about in this settlement. No sooner would he join me than a score of small children would come whooping by to splash in the creek. Or a miner would crash noisily through the willows to rinse a pan or seek a lost dog. I had to be remarkably quick to appear a passing stranger

to Jem whenever someone came near us. I could see that
the arrangement angered him, and he finally asked me
one day if I would not allow him to call at our hut and
ask my parents' permission to see me without conceal-
ment.

What a hope!

When I suggested that Jem might come to have a meal
with us one evening, that he would like to seek advice
from Father about mining, that he was a lonely orphan
who would so much appreciate an evening with a family,
my request was met with chilly silence. I was tempted
to add that he was the oldest son of an extremely wealthy
baronet, here only for a short time before returning to
claim his vast inheritances. But I feared that his rich
brogue would give that game away, and I could not be
sure that such wealth was to be had in Ireland. I fingered
the stupid strip of lace that Mama had brought all the
way out here with her to decorate the mantel over our
fireplace. It is a reminder of the gracious life she once
led, and I hate it. The dust and grime have to be carefully
laundered from it, and the heavy flatiron tears the stitches
as I press it, and it seems to me to be so *pitiful*! This is
not a lace place. But Mama will never face that fact, nor
I fear will my father.

"But why not, Papa? I only wish to offer him some
family hospitality. He is a thoroughly decent young man.
He saved me once from a great fright with some Indians."

"Some *what?*"

I hastened to explain that I had been on an errand,
had merely been surprised to see a group of Indian
gentlemen cooking their food, and that Jem had quietly
guided me away, lest some harm should befall me. I
made it sound a very dull occurrence, not a bit like the
exciting dash for safety and the sharp and intoxicating
conversation that I remembered.

They assured me that they considered only my wel-

fare, that the young man was so far beneath us in breed-
ing and education that it would be unfair to him to raise
his hopes of a friendship that could lead only to his
disappointment. I doubted that any of these arguments
would hold any sway with Jem, so with my finger tightly
enmeshed in the stupid lace I protested some more and
brought the wrath of both parents down on my head.
Mama shrieked that I was ruining her runner and hurried
across to free my finger and rescue her treasure. Then
she retired to her bed with the sad little strip clutched
to her bosom. Papa closed the matter by absolutely for-
bidding me ever to see or speak to "that fellow" again
nor ever to mention his name in the house. Then he
retired to the village, to salve his pride at the Royal Hotel.

After he had gone, Mama called me to her and begged
me to be more dutiful.

"I am sure your father will make a fortune here very
soon, dear," she murmured in her fading voice. "We
must both be patient, must we not?"

I thought not. It was all very well for her to be patient,
if she wished. Papa may have discussed with her his
decision to come to Australia, although I doubted that
he had. He certainly had not sought *my* approval, and I
can tell you such approval would not have been given!
The whole expedition had been a fool's mission, and I,
who was willing to make the best of it and find a friend
from among the few people available here, was asked to
be patient, be meek, be humble, like a piece of Turkey
carpet for others to walk on.

So I glibly promised my mother never to speak Jem's
name again in front of her or Papa and never to suggest
bringing him to the house. I took the piece of lace from
her hands and carefully replaced it on the mantel, then
sat by the fire for a while, glad that I had made poor
Mama happy. And even gladder that I had avoided prom-

ising some other things. I was quite resigned to never speaking his name and never asking them to have him in the house. I would try to discipline my wayward memory to forget him, and if it could not, how could I be blamed? I had *not* promised never to see him again, and I determined that I would see him whenever I was able to do so without upsetting my parents.

Next day I passed by Jem's mine, humming the tune we had arranged as our signal. It was the first few bars of an old Irish jig he had taught me, *The Irish Washerwoman*. Imagine mother playing *that* on her harp and father singing it with her! Such a *vulgar* tune.

Soon after I arrived at our meeting place by the ford, he came covered with dust and dirt.

"Well?" he asked, all smiles and hope.

"I had to promise never to speak your name again and never to invite you to visit our home," I told him near to tears.

"So," he said, lifting my chin with his grimy finger, "you see that you don't, my girl. You're in your parents' care till I'm in a position to take over from them. So see that you do as you're told. Don't go speaking my name nor asking me to your home. Promise?"

I promised.

"But do still be passing the mine from time to time. Will you be promising me that as well, Ann Bird?"

I made that promise gladly.

Sally

THERE was a dance in the woolshed at Pelican on Saturday night. Aunt Bessie spent all day in the kitchen baking sponge cakes and making sandwiches. The big Aga stove was throbbing with heat, and the table was covered with her cooking junk. She wouldn't have any of us in there to help, so Annie and I spent a quiet day, mostly in her room going through her wardrobe. After we'd fed the horses and the bulls, of course, and collected the eggs and tidied up the house. I was beginning to appreciate that life on a farm was no bed of roses!

The reason for going through Annie's gear was to decide what we were going to wear that night. I was all for wearing my second-best pair of jeans, but she said no, girls wore dresses mostly, and particularly *she* wore dresses to dances because her grandfather didn't like to see her in jeans, and if she had to wear a dress, then so did I. Nothing of hers fitted me, of course, so I settled for my denim skirt and a shirt we nicked from Cooper's room that she said he never wore anyway because he considered the material was too shiny and unmasculine. I tied it at the waist, and it was great, almost slimming in fact.

Then we got to work on her last summer's best and
lopped the skirt off until it was maxi enough to satisfy
Grandpa Cooper yet mini enough, almost, to satisfy Annie.
I stitched it up for her while she pressed my skirt; then
we had early baths, and just as well, because as soon as
Uncle James and the boys came in, there was a queue
for the bathroom and a lot of bad language because of
the hot-water shortage.

After a patchy dinner of warmed-up leftovers we were
ready to leave by seven o'clock. We all piled into the
station wagon, and this time, thank goodness, they left
the dogs at home because we each had a plate of food
on our knees, and the dogs' area at the back was occupied
by Davey, an icebox full of drinks, and boxes of rattling
china and glassware, each of which had a list of contents
stuck to its side in case of loss or theft. On top of all that
lay Uncle James's banjo case.

The homestead looked festive with lights on around
the verandas, but we drove right past it to the woolshed.
The big doors were open, and little white lights were
strung along the walls. Trestle tables were set up along
one wall, and we trundled in with our contributions to the
goodies supply and had a quick check of what had already
arrived. The boys filled the urn for Auntie Bess, and then
we stood waiting for the band to appear while Davey
tested the floor by sliding across it like a demented ice
skater. It didn't pass his test, so one of the men went
around with a white candle and a pocketknife, shaving
wax and spreading it around with the toe of his shoe.

Suddenly there was a lot of shouting and honking outside. The Berry boys from over the hill had arrived with
their four-wheel drive and trailer, and on the trailer was
tied an enormous upright piano. We all cheered and
helped to untie it, and the boys heaved it into the hall
and set it up in the corner.

"What you think of them? Anyone likely?" Annie whispered to me as we watched.

"The biggest Berry boy isn't bad."

"He's taken. Engaged to a pain in the neck from town. A manicurist. Second brother's all right."

The second brother was shorter even than me and what you might call stocky if you wanted to be kind about his shape.

"No thanks," I said, "I'll settle for that one who just came in. With the beard."

"Taken! Boy, you can pick them, Sal. Gorgeous, isn't he? But he's going steady with a girl from the bank. Talk about fat! She's enormous. She'll be along soon with a bunch of people from town."

I hadn't realized that Davey and Cooper had joined us, but Davey spoke up then. "I'll have you know, buster, that some of us blokes prefer our women with a bit of meat on them," he giggled, and he was so obviously quoting what someone had said to him that I turned to look at him just in time to see Cooper give him a hefty thump across the shoulders. And Cooper was looking quite embarrassed!

Before I could think of a smart remark to make, the band started up, and Cooper nodded in the direction of the dance floor.

"Give it a go?" he asked me.

"Why not," I agreed, since the biggest Berry boy and the handsome character with the beard were already spoken for.

He led me out onto the dance floor. The band had finished its warm-up, and I was just about to show him and the rest of them what I could do, when he grabbed me around the waist with one hand and with the other snatched my right hand and held it up in front of us. Then side by side we stalked up the room, with Davey chanting behind us.

"One, two, three, kick, back, two, three, stop." Then
Cooper swung me around and, while I was still spinning,
stepped forward and grabbed the girl in front of me. I
was left with only Davey in view, still chanting loudly.
"Spin her around and back, two, hi, four."

"What the hell kind of dance is this?" I hissed.

"Side . . . ways, barn . . . dance, waltz," he bellowed.
We waltzed for all of two seconds, then he lined me up
beside him as Cooper had and off we strode for our one-
two-three-kicks. It was the craziest dance I'd ever been
involved with, and by the time the music mercifully
stopped, I'd been guided, shoved, pushed, and spun by
every man on the floor, a few women who'd got up to
dance together since there weren't enough men game
enough to ask them, and one poor old guy who'd just
been leaning against the wall quietly watching until
I came reeling out of the crowd. He very politely,
and silently, steered me around his bit of the dance,
then sent me whirling back into the melee again. I tell
you, if I could have stopped that darn music for long
enough, I would have grabbed that Cooper Cooper and
pummeled him to death right there in the middle of that
bouncing woolshed. But there were so many people
on the floor, and others joining in all the time, that I
didn't even get around to dancing *(dancing?)* with him
again.

When it was over, I staggered to the buffet, collected
a glass of punch, and collapsed on one of the benches
by the door. Annie came up glowing, the handsome guy
with the beard following along behind.

"How'd you like that?" She could surely have known
how I'd liked it by the way my eyes were rolling and the
way I was slumped exhausted on that bench. "Great one
to break the ice, isn't it?"

I had to agree. The heat and all those pounding feet
would surely have shattered the iceberg that sunk the

Titanic, but I was grateful to her for hauling a man along for me to meet.

I wasn't grateful for long. In spite of the neat beard, that must have been the most taciturn guy I had ever encountered. He just stood there, missing his fat girl-friend, I guess, while I floundered about trying to make small talk. When the band started up again, he asked me to dance, and that was better because we didn't look quite so stupid stumping around the hall without saying a word to each other. Well, we probably did look stupid, but I felt a tad better, and he wasn't all that bad as a dancer.

The band improved as the night wore on. At the beginning there was Uncle James with his banjo, a man with a trombone, both of those quite good, and Grandpa Cooper on the piano, quite appallingly bad. Mind you, that piano had had a rough night, being hauled across country on a trailer behind a four-wheel drive. If it was out of tune, who could blame it? But after a while there was a commotion at the door, and a man staggered in lugging a huge drum kit, followed by a trumpeter and a saxophone player. So the noise increased, and the quality of the music would have too, if it hadn't been for Grandpa Cooper, who seemed to take quite a pride in being the one with the slowest beat and therefore the last to finish each time. He even gave the impression of sometimes launching into an entirely different tune.

Good old Auntie Bess came to the rescue, of course. She moved across to the piano and very sweetly began to murmur to the pianist, obviously asking if she could have a go. Grandpa Cooper held out as long as he could, but he was finally worn down by his daughter-in-law's persistence and vacated the piano stool for her. I guess she and Uncle James had played a bit together, because they kept the beat going well and even slipped in a few modern tunes that a person could actually *dance* to, I mean without having to hang on to a partner like grim death to avoid being trampled underfoot by the stamping hordes.

I had to endure three dances with the beard simply because I couldn't think of any way to get rid of him. It seemed too mean to just walk away and leave him standing there, and you couldn't say he was offensive in any way. I mean he *looked* adorable, and he didn't say enough to cause any problems. Actually it suited me to stand around with him between dances anyway, because I might have been standing alone otherwise; certainly no one else showed the slightest interest in me—except for Davey, who stood against the far wall and leered at me, wiggling his eyebrows up and down in a very juvenile way.

During our third dance I noticed that my partner had become even quieter than usual, sort of tense, so I looked around the hall, and sure enough a group of people had just come in, and one of them was a plump and jolly girl a bit older than me. He was too polite, thank goodness, to abandon me right away, but as soon as the dance was over he said a brisk "Cheerio" and hurried across to her. She didn't seem all that fat to me. Annie exaggerates terribly sometimes. I drifted over as nonchalantly as I could to sit beside Grandpa Cooper, who was still eyeing the piano wistfully.

Choosing my words carefully, I thanked him for playing so *long* for us and fetched him a glass of punch; then I settled in to question him about the past history of the area.

He didn't know much about it, except that there had been a settlement there during the gold rush.

"Quite a sizable little town, actually. Lot of gold around

these parts, you know, so they came from all over the world for it. Mind you, our family was here earlier. The first Cooper came across the mountains in the eighteen forties. A remarkable chap, by all acounts. Sailed out on one of those American clipper ships; they were the fastest, you know." (I hadn't known, of course.) "Must have been a grand experience, on the deck of one of those fully rigged beauties, flying through the roaring forties to settle in a new land." (Grand! Pretty wet too, I imagine!) "Sometimes covered four hundred sea miles a day, although I have heard that the masters fudged the figures sometimes to win the cargo contracts. Speed was important in those days, you know."

I was about to tell him that speed was pretty important these days too, particularly to me who only had another week to solve my little mystery, but he drifted back onto the subject of the settlement without any prompting.

"Hard to imagine how they managed, isn't it? No comforts then, poor things. No running water, electricity, motor cars, no doctors, lawyers, or parsons. But half the poor beggars could neither read nor write. And what the women must have endured . . ."

I feared our conversation was developing into one of those I frequently had with my own grandfather. A "you young people don't appreciate how lucky you are; in my day we *really* had it hard" type monologue that I found *really* boring, because it's not our fault we weren't there to suffer along with them. So I looked acutely interested, as I did with Grandpa Sloane, and said in my most sincere and intense voice, "Oh yes, Mr. Cooper. I do agree. It must have been *ghastly*, and were there many people living here, then?" Ever so cunningly changing the subject, you see.

"Thousands, I believe. There were twenty thousand

people in Gulgong in the eighteen seventies, you know. Pelican was never as big as—"

"You mean the village was Pelican too?"

"First. It was the first Pelican Creek. My ancestor called his holding 'Hampshire,' which was pretty pretentious of him, when you come to think of it, but he'd come from there, d'y'see? Anyway, the miners called the place Pelican Creek; don't ask me why—there certainly weren't any pelicans around—and later, when the gold had finished and the miners had gone, the family changed the name to Pelican Creek. Then, when we parceled it out later, the main property stayed as Pelican, and the boys called theirs by the names they'd always had, 'Four Mile' for four-mile paddock and 'Hillside' for the land on the side of the hill, where you're staying at the moment. And let me tell you how very happy we are to have you here, my dear. Any friend—any daughter of a friend of young Bess is a friend of mine. Salt of the earth, young Bess."

And she was, too, pounding away at the piano there, red faced, hair flying, and turning to smile all the time at the people bopping past.

"Thanks, Mr. Cooper. That's awfully interesting. Is there anywhere I can read up about the early days? I'd love to know more." And especially what happened to Jem Ever and Ann Bird, whoever they were. But I didn't tell him that.

Then as he stood up to be the first in for supper, he really gave me a shock. "Best one to ask about the history of these parts is young Cooper. Junior. Cooper there." I glanced quickly at the dancers, and there was young Cooper. Junior, Cooper there, dancing in a most devout way with a skinny girl with long black hair and far too much makeup.

"Cooper? *That* Cooper?" I gaped.

"That Cooper." He smiled. "Knows more about this part of the world than anyone, I reckon. Ask him. He'll tell you. Now, let's go and collect some sustenance, eh?"

I followed him to the trestle tables, wondering if it was going to be worthwhile asking Cooper some questions and not looking forward to having him brush me off again.

Ann

MY poor mama is gravely ill. She lies in her bed all day, pale and sad, and I can feel her drifting slowly and inevitably away from us.

All the foolish possessions she had insisted on bringing with her seem right and necessary now. I take her bonnets from their boxes and try them on to show her how fashionable they will be on our return to civilization. Carefully I launder and iron her precious scraps of lace and fashion them into collars for her frail shoulders, and she smiles for me and sits a little straighter on her pillow. But soon the pain comes back, and she coughs, and droops, and finally sleeps again.

I have come to know the tiny woman who wears her husband's hat and has seven children, the baker's wife. They all lived in a tent when they first arrived but now have a tiny dwelling built of bark with a big kitchen at the back and a counter in the front room, with fresh loaves on display at a price of twopence each. Their chimney is the biggest in the settlement, of course, and on cold days groups of children as well as their own gather around it for warmth and play happily there for hours. I am convinced they need a school here, but it could never be so cosy or pleasant as the meeting place by the baker's oven.

She's a gossipy little thing with a willing ear, and I heard myself telling her of Mama's illness one day, even though I know that Papa would prefer that I did not mention it. He seems to feel that people will not think well of us if they know, and yet one can hardly blame poor Mama for her malady, and the baker's wife is very sympathetic.

"Listen, love, the name's Prew, Jane Prew, and you can call me Jane."

I dared not tell her to call me Ann because of Father, so I carefully addressed her as Mrs. Prew, and she seemed to like it, and I am now Miss Shipton, so that was easily done, thank goodness. I would not like to earn the wrath of Mrs. Prew, and as in all our chats she never makes mention of Papa, I presume she has not forgiven him yet for calling her his "good woman"! Some days when she has time, she bakes a delicate pastry for Mama and will not let me pay her for it, and she has told me of a couple who live on the far side of the hill who have bought cows from the local squatter and might sell me some milk.

I found the place easily yesterday, my nose and ears guided there with no difficulty at all. Cows, pigs, and fowls all jostled about for space in a tiny yard where the filth was indescribable, but I ventured in and knocked on the door, keeping poor Mama in my mind so that I could not retreat.

A skinny woman answered the door and insisted that I come inside. I did but immediately wished that I had not because the air was even stronger there, with the smell of the large dish of cream that she was beating into butter with a wooden spoon. It had begun to separate, and the yellow cream was lumpy in a sea of bluish buttermilk. She scattered a handful of salt on it and sat down to beat some more.

"Can't afford to waste any of it, love," she gasped as she fought against the stubborn butterfat. "We sells the milk and we sells the eggs, then what milk don't sell we covers and sets till the cream settles, then I scoops it off and sells that. What cream don't sell I set some more, then makes into butter like this, and sells that. And what's left I feed to the pigs. Then when himself's got time to kill one, I cures the bacon and sells it."

With all this commercial dealing I would have expected a much grander farm and a more robust mistress of it. But she was pale, gaunt, and slow moving, and I wished she would serve herself some of the nourishment that her farm offered. However, I had no time to organize her better health and was all too eager to escape from the place for the sake of my poor, suffering nose. I had her fill my pannikin with milk, regretted I had no money for eggs, and promised to come again when I could afford to buy more.

Mama was sweetly grateful for the warm drink I made her but could not take much of it, and I fear the change in diet has come too late to help her. Yet there are times when she rallies and seems more like her old self.

This morning, for instance, a bullock dray came lumbering up the hillside, laden with supplies for the general store and liquor for the hotels. I saw it coming as I stood in our doorway, and heard the crack of the stockwhip and the bullocky's shouts, and I sent up a most devout and heartfelt prayer that mail from England was included in its cargo.

A packet of mail was there for us, and I ran all the way back to mother, my fingers tingling from touching it. There were letters of business for Papa and two from Grandmama in London.

Mama slit them open and we read them together, long letters full of love and delight at our good fortune! Grandmama said how wonderful it was that we were heading off across the mountains to settle in such delightful surroundings as Bathurst seemed to be, and how clever of Papa to choose such a fertile sheep property with such a comfortable home for Mama and me! What was the servant situation; surely we did not have to make do with convicts? Which flowers would we have blooming in our garden, and had the fashion for shorter skirts taken on in New South Wales?

I was undecided whether to laugh or cry by the time I had finished reading them, and so, judging from her expression, was Mama.

"She has not received our last letters," she murmured in a thoughtful tone.

But it was more than that. Grandmama was under a much stronger impression than any letters from Mama or myself could have given her. To be sure, when we had written from Sydney, our plans did not include taking part in a gold rush! My father had spoken to agents and had traveled alone as far as Bathurst to look at likely properties to buy. He found one hundred acres of suitable land and arranged with a carpenter for a house to be built on it at a cost of one hundred and twenty pounds. A house much grander than the one we now occupied, with a separate kitchen, proper doors, and windows with glass, and a wooden ceiling to the parlor.

So we had prepared to settle near Bathurst, although I would have loved to stay in Sydney and a small house near our lodgings in Camperdown would have suited me well. The magnificent buildings of St. Paul's and St. John's colleges of the University were nearby. The city itself was a short trip away on the omnibus, with fine banks and warehouses, the imposing Museum and the dear little Church of St. James, which Mama and I attended, the elaborate new Town Hall and Post Office almost completed, the gardens of the Domain, the pleasant walk and beautiful views from Mrs. Macquarie's Chair by Government House, the movement of shipping at the Circular Quay and Darling Harbour, and, best of all for me, a Free Public Library and School of Arts.

And here we were now, a long way from the comfort of a small farm a few miles out of Bathurst town and even farther from the delights of Sydney because Papa had gambled away his money and contracted gold fever! I looked around at the meanness of our bark hut, and as my eyes returned to my mother, they met hers coming back the same way. We gazed at each other for a moment, then each began to laugh. The difference between our present situation and the fond dreams of my grandmother was so extreme! But beneath my laughter was a strong resentment of what my father had done.

Later, while Mama slept, still smiling at the memory of words from home, I crept out of the house and went for a walk across the ford and up the hill toward the Chinaman's garden. I had no money left to buy vegetables, but it was a pleasant walk leading to the grand house of the squatter. I did not go that far but turned humming *The Irish Washerwoman* and retraced my steps to the ford.

He came soon and sat beside me on the grass beneath the willow.

"You're looking pensive, Ann Bird," he said. "What's happened to you, then?"

I told him of my mother's illness and our letters from my sadly misled grandmama. "It's all Papa's fault. He's been writing to my grandparents and telling them great tales of sheep properties and comfortable living and how well he is doing here on the money they gave him to come, and all the while their daughter is dying there. She's dying, Jem. And I don't know what to do for her."

He stroked my hair until I was quiet. "Can't blame your dad, though, really. There's a lot of us thought to make our fortunes with the gold. He's no worse than the rest of us, girl. Maybe he'll strike it rich, *then* get you your farm at Bathurst."

"I don't want a farm at Bathurst!" I whimpered. "I want to live in Sydney. No, I don't. I want to live back in Bloomsbury, where there are books, and concerts, and operas. Well, I haven't actually been to a concert or an opera yet, but the books and the Museum . . . Oh, Jem, I want to go home!"

I really was quite disgustingly maudlin for a time, but I managed to pull myself together and asked if he had received any mail. He seemed surprised that I should think he would and pretended gruffly not to care.

"That bullocky, though, that brought your mail, I know that fellow well. Came over the range with him last year. What a trip that was. You know I don't think the man or his offsider was sober for one tiny step of the way!"

I had noticed many hotels on the route when we had come in the fine carriage that my father had thought fitting for us to leave Sydney in, but to be nonsober *all* the way was remarkable.

"I swear it! Thing was, they had a load of kegs on board for the hotels up here, along with the tables and chairs and the beds and the gold cradles and the windlasses and the picks and the shovels, and on the first night out of Sydney, just past Parramatta there, they got to the kegs and performed a very interesting operation."

I waited, wondering.

"They unyoked the bulls and turned them out to graze for the night, hobbled their horses to keep them close to the camp, while I lit the fire and set up hammocks by the back wheels of the wagon. Then they—"

"Why did they need horses when they had perfectly good bulls to do the work?"

"To muster the bulls next morning—they'll go miles for their feed, bulls will. And to *ride*, girl! To ride! Now, let me go on with the story with no more interruptions, eh? After all this they set to with a sharp gimlet and bored a hole into one of the barrels at the top under the brand mark, and another at the bottom where some more words were printed there. Then they had to be pretty nippy to hold a bucket under the bottom hole to catch the flow of the hard stuff. When they'd broached enough to get each of them through the night and the next day, they'd hammer a tiny peg into each of the holes, tap it well in so's it was flush with the rest of the barrel, and burn over the ends of the pegs with a bit of iron they'd heated in the camp-fire. Every night they did this, each night a different keg. Kept them very happy it did, all the way here, and the publicans never noticed, or if they did, they never said. Tapping the keg, they called it."

"That's disgusting, Jem, really disgusting!"

He shrugged. " 'Tis hard work, crashing and smashing up and down those hills with a team of stubborn animals and a loaded dray. A dangerous job too, Ann Bird. Once those creatures stop, it's mighty hard to get them moving again, and just you think about a steep downhill run."

I thought about it. "They'd make up some time then, wouldn't they?"

"They would not, you fool woman. The bullockies I was with trailed great logs behind to slow the bulls down, even unhitched some of the animals. But then a wheel might break, an axle give way. I tell you, those bullockies did well on their stolen drop of spirits—and now, Ann Bird, I've a favor to ask of you."

He took a clean but tattered kerchief from the pocket of his trousers and opened it on the grass between us. It contained a tidy collection of coins, and in with them sparkled a small diamond pin such as my father used to wear on his cravat, except that my father's was larger. I wondered who wore my father's pin now.

"Will you take care of it for me, Ann? 'Tis not safe in the tent I share. Not that the men are thieves, you understand, but I'll not be putting temptation in their way, now that the hotels are stocked with grog. The pin belonged to my father; it was his only treasure, and the money I saved myself."

So I stowed his fortune carefully in the pocket of my apron and set off across the ford.

I hid it in the bottom of my cabin trunk beneath the useless finery I had brought, then set about preparing the evening meal.

When Papa came in, he sifted through his letters, read some, and tossed others aside; they were the accounts, no doubt. Then Mama handed him those she had received from her mother.

"What a foolish woman she is," he exclaimed when he had read them. "I merely told her we were *considering* a place at Bathurst. Will she not be delighted when she hears we have made our fortune from gold? Eh, Mary?"

Grandmama might be delighted, but I would be flabbergasted when that happened! So far Papa had gleaned from his mine only enough gold to keep us fed, and that sparingly. But he held Mother's hand for a while, so I could not chastise him; then he left us and went to the hotel, and I regretted my kind thoughts. I know it is wicked of me; I am an undutiful daughter, but he has let us down so often.

I heard Papa come lurching in late that night, and later still, when he and Mama were gone to sleep, I heard a faint whistling outside the hut. It was the first few bars of *The Irish Washerwoman*! I lay very still until I was sure, then quietly slipped out of bed, wriggled my feet into my boots, wrapped my eiderdown about my shoulders, and crept through the main room and out of the house.

Jem was waiting beneath the big gum tree.

"Here," he whispered, " 'tis some eggs for your mother." He thrust a bundle into my hands.

"Where did you get them?" I whispered back through my chattering teeth.

"Just happened upon 'em. Walking along, minding my business, and there they were beside the track. Some wandering hen must have laid them there, and wasn't it lucky I came upon 'em?"

"Jem! I've never seen any wandering hens around here. Anyone who has a hen keeps it well under guard."

"Well, this one got away, didn't it then? A proud little layer it was, and running free! Rejoice for it and make a healthy omelette for your poor mother. And now inside you go, Ann Bird, before you catch your death."

He bundled me and the contraband eggs back inside the hut, and the next day I cooked an omelette for Mama. She did enjoy it so much and never once asked where the eggs had come from.

Sally

WE arrived home from the dance at about three in the morning, the last to leave because Aunt Bess had promised so many requests on the piano that she could have played until well into the next day, and probably would have cheerfully if Uncle James hadn't resolutely packed his banjo in the case and snatched the poor drummer's sticks away from him in mid bash.

She still insisted on giving us a round of *Auld Lang Syne* backed up by the trombone player and the trumpeter, both a trifle unsteady on their feet and slapdash with their notes. Everyone joined in a sort of general romp around the woolshed and shouted and stamped and kissed their partners. Grandpa and Davey each grabbed an arm and hauled me on to the floor, and it was rather fun really, and I shouted and stamped with the best of them and kissed both of my partners when it was over. And I meant it sincerely; they are so like each other and so sweet.

Then we had to help avert a nervous prostration by Davey, who had trouble counting all the stuff to make it tally with the labels he'd stuck on the boxes. At last he narrowed down the missing articles to one cup and one plate, so while he was frantically searching behind benches and under tables, I nicked one of each from someone else's box. Honestly, we could have been there all night!

Then we couldn't find Annie, so we all roamed around calling her, the others quietly, me in what you might call stentorian tones. If Annie was with a boy somewhere, then she'd need a noisy warning from a friend before she was sprung by one of her parents. Sure enough, she emerged blinking from the front seat of the Berry boys' four-wheel drive along with the third Berry boy. This one, although shorter than the biggest Berry boy, wasn't as plump as the second Berry boy and had possibilities that I hadn't noticed before. Crafty old Annie hadn't bothered to draw them to my attention either.

Then we had to find Cooper. By the way he'd been trailing around after the dark-haired skinny girl with all the makeup on they'd probably eloped and were halfway to Sydney by now. So I didn't bother joining in that search but climbed into the back of the station wagon with Davey and helped him tote up his lists once more. Annie joined us and immediately pretended to be asleep so that I couldn't question her in front of Davey. Finally the others arrived, Cooper all virtue because he had not, in fact, been running off with that female but had been down by the sheep pens with Grandpa, examining a broken fence or something. Really, country people are *weird*!

So we arrived home about three in the morning and I did think we might have a sleep-in next day. But no. Everyone was milling around at dawn crack, and it was off to church for the whole family.

It was a pleasant little church, set in a corner of a paddock, with a cluster of houses and a general store around it. After the service we all stood about in groups and chatted with the neighbors, although most of them had been at the dance the night before so I was surprised that anyone had anything left to talk about.

There was a graveyard beside the church. I was tempted to wander in and have a look at the old gravestones, but I didn't want to be missing when it was time to go home to eat, so I strolled over to talk to Grandpa Cooper instead. With a small ulterior motive, I must admit.

"You must know just about every family that ever lived here, Mr. Cooper."

"I certainly do, young lady. You name me a name, and I can tell you all about them. I guarantee you that."

But his guarantee was useless, because he'd never heard of a family called Ever, although he was familiar with the Everetts. They had come to the area just after World War Two, as soldier settlers, lived close to town, and had no connection with Pelican, Hillside, or Four Mile as far as he knew. The darling man made no inquiries as to why I was so interested in the local families, so I let him go on about the Everetts, although the name on the brooch was definitely Ever, and therefore no connection at all. Then he gave me a rundown on the Chans. Dr. Chan's family was one of the wealthiest in the district and they'd been among the first arrivals, but again it had nothing to do with my discovery.

I glanced again at the graveyard, wondering if I could possibly fit in a quick dash to read some names, but Uncle James chose to rally the troops at that moment, and we all had to pile into the car again to drive home. A pity, as it happened.

Sunday dinner was one of Aunt Bess's specialties, and we ate ourselves into an absolute stupor with roast lamb and heaps of veggies, and apple-pie and cream to follow. Then we four kids washed up while the olds lolled about reading the Sunday papers, and after that Davey suggested a walk.

"Hey. Let's go to the creek first," he ordered. "I want to show Sally the ford."

The others were lethargic after their late night and early morning and big dinner, so Davey had his way and we set off toward the creek. We walked across the home paddock to the spot where I had fallen down the shaft, and the four of us stood around the hole to stare in. I was embarrassed. It really wasn't deep at all. I *could* have jumped out of it if I'd tried, almost, and the fuss I'd made seemed pretty stupid in the light of day. But the others were decent about it and abstained from mentioning all the trouble they'd had to go to to haul me out of it, so I thought it best to snigger a bit and say how things always seemed so much worse in the dark.

"Hey, don't they though?" Davey agreed. "I'd have been scared witless too, if it'd been me."

"Well, I didn't say I was exactly *witless*, Davey," I protested. "What's that down the bottom there? Looks like a slab of rock or something."

"It is a slab of rock," said Cooper. "Come on." And he set off down the hill toward the creek.

There were flat stones set in the bed of the creek. Useful to cross by when there was some water there no doubt, but not needed at the moment, for the creek consisted of a few muddy puddles with great patches of sand and rocks between. But we all stepped carefully across by the ford, as Davey insisted, and made our way up the other side.

I glanced back. There were willows on the bank, cool and frondy, and I could imagine that it would be a most delightful spot to linger when the creek was flowing with clean water and the grass was green.

I caught up with the others at the spot where Cooper said the old township had been. If he hadn't told me, I would never have suspected! A few piles of biggish stones marked where chimneys had once stood, but there wasn't even a track to show a street, let alone any curbing or guttering.

"This bigger chimney would have been the baker's oven," Cooper told us, "and we think the forge was probably here."

He didn't make any impression on me. I mean, there wasn't anything there *now*, except a few old stones, yet he went on about it as if it really mattered that a few mad miners had camped there for a while about a hundred years ago.

"There's quite a group of us now interested in local history," he said, "but unfortunately there just aren't any records available about this settlement. Gulgong's lucky, they had a guy named Holtermann who came out from England and he took photographs of just about everything in the town, but here there's nothing."

"Right, Cooper," I said. "Let's move on. And by the way, since you know so much about life around these parts, how come you don't know about the Evers?"

"Hey, sounds like something you catch, like the measles."

"Sally, *why* do you keep on about the Evers? We *told* you. No one's ever heard of them."

"Hey, Annie, *ever* heard! Get it?"

"Oh, do pipe down, David. I can't remember where I heard the name, Annie. Mr. and Mrs. Ever, Cooper, do they feature in your local history at all?"

Now if I had had the sense to say *Jem* Ever, I might have found out much more and much sooner, but no, dummy that I was, I still wanted to keep something back, so I asked about Mr. and Mrs. Ever, and Cooper, with all his historical knowledge, had to admit that he'd never heard of such a family.

We drifted down the other side of the hill, and there was the creek again. It had curved around, and now we were standing beneath a huge gum tree with an ancient elm nearby. I was tired from all the walking, so I lay down in the shade, and the others finally joined me. Reluctantly. They're an energetic lot, the Coopers, and even as he settled Davey brought with him a handful of stones to shy at a nearby stump.

"Oh, David, do leave the poor thing alone. It looks so lonely somehow, all by itself there."

Funnily enough, I'd been thinking the same thing, so I sided with Annie and we persuaded Davey to stop. He persisted in fiddling with the stones and suddenly Cooper muttered: "Mullock." He dragged us all up again to go and look at the spot where Davey had collected his stones.

"Mullock. That's a mullock heap, useless stones, no gold in them, and this was where they had the puddling machine to separate the pebbles from the clay."

I could actually see a sort of hollow in the grass where he was pointing and there was a small pile of whitish stones there, but I couldn't imagine what a puddling machine could look like and thought Cooper was making rather too much of it. I mean, it wasn't as if there was an old ruined castle, or anything you could actually *look* at.

To tell you the truth, I was feeling completely fed up. I'd been banished to the country for almost a week now, and neither of my parents had given me a thought. Ma had telephoned the night I arrived to check that I'd made it safely. Traveling all that distance alone in a train was more than I could manage according to her, and she'd been frantic because boarders at our school left earlier than day girls, so Annie was already at home by the time they decided to shoot me up to the farm.

Now I was beginning to wonder if they had decided to cut off all communications completely. I left the others and started off back to the house because suddenly I rather wanted to be by myself.

I made it to the ford across the creek, and then I had

to stop because my eyes were beginning to sting. I guess I must be allergic to something about the country. Anyway, I sat down on the bank beneath the willow to consider my position and that of Ma and Pa. Being lumbered with a sixteen-year-old daughter, and a fat one at that, was probably holding them back more than they would admit. I cost a lot to feed and clothe and educate, as Pa is always telling anyone who'll listen, but then so is every father of every other person I know. They have to queue up to get their hard-luck stories told when they get together. But if it's such a general problem, why isn't every other couple fighting all the time like my parents?

I heard the others coming, so I quickly turned on to my stomach so that my eyes wouldn't be seen and pretended to be dozing.

"Hey, Sal, you okay?"

"Lazy slob!"

Davey and Annie passed across the stones. Cooper said nothing and began to cross, then stepped back and sat down on the grass beside me. If there'd been any water at all in the stupid creek, I swear I would have pushed him in and held his head under for one hour or two to teach him to mind his own business.

He didn't say anything for a long while, time enough for me to blink a few times and do a few surreptitious sniffs. Then: "Pleasant here," he said. "It's one of my favorite spots. I like to think of the people who lived up there coming down here to be peaceful, to get away from the noise and dust of the diggings."

I nodded, touched by his sentiments, but then he added, "Truth is, though, they probably used the creek for everything—washing, bathing, et cetera. Likewise their animals, I guess. A sort of community water hole. My trouble is I make it sound all rosy, when probably it was as sordid as hell."

"No you don't, Cooper. I think it's great, the way you're interested in them and how they lived and all that. It's wonderful that someone like you cares about them."

Cooper looked surprised, and I was startled myself. I hadn't really thought Cooper was doing anything special when he started rabbiting on about history, but here, in this cool and quiet place, my feelings suddenly changed. I was grateful to him for caring, and fonder of him than I'd ever felt before. So I did what I hadn't been able to do so far: told someone about the trouble my family was going through. I told Cooper about the silences and the fights and me having to deliver messages between them, and the reason I'd come to Hillside, because Ma and Pa obviously thought I was going mad or something and couldn't cope.

"Thing is, Coop, I really can't. Cope. I mean I don't know which side I'm on from one day to the next."

"You don't have to be on any side, so far as I can see." He broke a small branch from the willow and used it to fan the flies off both of us. I don't know why it is, but no matter how idyllic a place is there always seems to be a battalion of flies who've found it first and think they own it.

"I mean, can't you concede they've each got a point and leave it at that? Strikes me there's not often a right and wrong involved in these things. Each side's a bit right and a bit wrong, if you see what I mean. *And* pretty damn selfish, both of them, if it comes to that."

"Oh, I don't know." Fact is, I was beginning to think that they *had* been pretty selfish. I mean they'd been snapping and silencing and filling the house with bad vibes for months now and I hadn't said a word, yet the moment I blew up, they bunged me off out of the place.

"Know what I reckon?" Cooper leaned forward. I'd

turned around to face him once we'd begun to talk, and he leaned right forward and for a mad moment I thought he was going to MAKE ADVANCES! But all he did was flick a bit of leaf off my cheek, a bit that had fallen off his fly switch. "I reckon it's time you started to think of yourself as you. Not part of a threesome, but *you*. Sally Matthews. Herself. In her own right. Let your parents do what they want to with their lives, but you get stuck into planning and living your own. What are you, sixteen?"

"And a bit. Three months."

"Well, there you are then, you see. Old enough to make a few decisions of your own. You've got a brain in there. You're not bad looking. . . ."

"Well, thank you, I'm sure!"

"That's okay. You're pretty much average, and there's a lot to be said for us average blokes. Average covers most of the world's population, if you think about it for a minute. It's sort of comfortable, being average."

I didn't particularly want to ponder too long on my being average, it was a bit too close to mediocre for my liking, but I knew that poor Cooper was trying to help.

He wasn't allowed to offer any more character diagnoses, however, because Davey appeared on the other side of the creek, red faced from having run all the way back from the house.

"Hey, Sal!" he bellowed. "Mum says you gotta come home. Your mum and dad have telephoned, and they're gonna ring back. Hey, come on, willya? Get a wriggle on!"

So I did.

Ann

TODAY was a day of surprises and shocks.

This morning I was interrupted by a visit from the squatter's son. And he was not very welcome, I can tell you. There I was, with a big pan of melted mutton fat on the fire, dipping into it wicks I had cut from an old woollen skirt, hanging them up to dry, dipping them again as soon as they had set, then again and again until they were thick enough to be useful, hot and flustered and clad in my oldest gingham and furious at having to make the stupid candles that never did burn well. They were far too soft and had to be snuffed frequently, but since the butcher is a religious man, and sympathetic to my mother, the mutton fat is free.

So that is the state I was in when someone knocked. I hung the candle I was dipping and opened the door. There stood Charles with a red kerchief in his hand.

"Good morning, Miss Ann." He blushed and squirmed as if I were a dragon, and with the heat of the fire and my annoyance, perhaps I resembled one at that. "I heard that your mother was ill, so I brought you some eggs from my mother's hens."

Mother was sleeping, so I thought it best not to invite

him inside, but I took the eggs, thankful for any help that might come our way, resentful that we should require it, and regretful that he had not brought candles. "I shall call and thank your mother for them," I offered, and immediately he began to shuffle.

"Please! Don't! She doesn't . . . I didn't . . . Please don't thank her. She really dislikes to be thanked!"

So I promised *not* to thank his mother for the eggs, and we stood there with nothing more to say. After what seemed to me to be close to three hours, he spoke again.

"I would have brought more, but our hens don't seem to be laying very well lately. Fewer eggs than usual, you know."

Indeed I did know. Regular deliveries of eggs had been made at dead of night by Jem, and now I realized that his generous little "vagabond hen" was in fact a resident of the squatter's fowl yard.

"I've heard that hens can be unpredictable," I said, keeping a straight face with difficulty. "Thank you, and now I must get back to my candles."

He looked inside the room and saw my pitiful little rows of dripping fat hanging from the rafters.

"There is a device that makes them more easily, you know," he murmured.

"I *know* there is." I snapped at him. "I happen to *enjoy* making them this way!"

If I had had a candle in my hand, I would have thrown it at him, but the eggs I was holding were too precious to waste. We glared at each other for a moment, then he coolly said, "Well, Miss Shipton, I am very happy for you then. Please wish your mother well for me. Goodbye."

And he walked away, leaving me glaring after him, angry at his superior tone and not even grateful for the eggs. I was near to being embarrassed by the number of eggs that I had, hidden under my bed!

Later in the morning he returned carrying a queer tin contraption, a tray with cylindrical tubes set into it. He handed it to me and said solemnly, "I do apologize for my rudeness to you this morning, Miss Shipton. I know how worried you must be at your mother's illness. I also apologize for depriving you of some pleasure. I know you delight in forming candles by the old method, but I beg you to try this means of making them."

He came inside and set the tray down on the table. I was inclined to keep him out, but he strode in so purposefully that I was forced to back in myself, and Mother was up and sitting in the armchair by the table, so there was little I could do that would not appear churlish. They greeted each other like old friends, and Charles then proceeded to show us both how to manage his candle maker. After the wicks were inserted, melted tallow was to be poured into the tin tray whence it would run into the tubes until they were full. Then tiny slivers of wood were set in to keep the wicks taut. When the tallow was cool, the wood was removed and the candles taken out of the mold.

"How very kind of your dear mama to lend it to us," my mother said.

"Please! Do not think of thanking her! She has no further need of it. We have lamps. . . . She doesn't . . . I didn't . . ."

From his fluster I could tell that his mother knew no more about the candle maker than she had known about the eggs. I really was extremely angry at his patronizing charity, but I could not stop myself from laughing at his clumsiness. I turned away to conceal my giggles, and poor dear Mama said, "What is it, Ann dear? Oh, don't be upset. The young man is so kind to us, try not to cry."

I tried, very hard, but he came to my side and saw that I was laughing. He watched me in silence for a moment; then he whispered, "I'm not very good at this, am I? I know that my mother would be very happy . . . We want you to . . . I want to . . . I think perhaps I should go now. Do please let me know if there is anything at all that I can do to assist you. Please?"

I nodded with my lips pressed tightly together in case I should embarrass Mama, and saw him out the door.

"I think that young man fancies you, Ann dear." Mama said.

"He may fancy what he chooses," I gloomed as I examined our new device. "I don't fancy him. And I don't fancy this either. Stupid contraption!"

But I shall try the candle maker. It has possibilities.

When Father came home, he brought news of a strike! Not his own, of course; I had given up hoping for that. In fact, he arrived home so clean these nights that I doubted he ever went down his own mine at all. More probably he spent his time telling the other miners how to work *their* claims! Tonight, however, I listened with delight to his gossip, because the finder of the gold was known to me.

"That young Irish chap, you know, Mary, the insolent fellow who pestered Ann at the dance. It seems he found a decent-sized nugget today. No doubt he has sold it already to the bank and drunk the proceeds. The price is three pounds sixteen shillings an ounce at the moment. Could have set him up for some time, but you know what those Irish are. Completely feckless."

Feckless! My feckless father, who had gambled away all his money *and* the property he was to purchase at Bathurst, along with *his* father's diamond pin before we had even left Sydney! And he was calling Jem feckless! I was itching to argue with him, but before I could assemble the right words, there was a knock on the door.

I rushed to answer it in case it was someone I knew, but my father was there before me. He opened the door and said nothing. I heard Jem's voice.

"Mr. Shipton! I've struck it! I've brought the grandest nugget in the world to show you. May I come in?"

"Indeed you may not, sir."

"But just to show you . . ."

My father turned impatiently away and shut the door. Mother, suspecting I think where most of her eggs were coming from, tried a small rebellion.

"My dear, I really do feel we should let the boy in for a moment, to congratulate him on his good fortune."

"Mary!"

"I'm sure there is no harm in him. Quite a pleasant lad."

"*Mary!*"

The second *Mary* was enough. The rebellion was put down, as Mother's rebellions always were.

There was another knock on the door. I really thought that my father would have a fit as he strode over to open it again. There was so much unease in the air, I thought anything might happen.

This time Jem spoke louder, and with anger. "Mr. Shipton. I wish to speak to your daughter."

Of course that was just the very worst way to approach Father. Even I would hesitate to use such an aggressive tone of voice, but how was Jem to know? My father answered him in his most clipped, British manner, which contrasted so greatly with Jem's rich, careless brogue.

"How dare you, sir! Away with you, and if I ever see you near my home again I promise to give you a whipping you will not forget!"

I knew that he meant it. So I went to the doorway and stood beside my father. I saw Jem in the light from my candles, standing very still, with such a look of fury on his face that I was afraid of what he and my father might do to each other. He held out his hand to me. Lying on his palm was a nugget of gold measuring more than an inch across and glowing with richness even though it had only our dim candlelight to reflect.

"Look!" Jem shouted. "I found it today. For you, Ann Bird. Will you take it?"

I heard Mother gasp behind us. Father stood very still beside me, but with the stillness of a dangerous snake making ready to strike.

"Congratulations, sir," I finally managed. "We are very pleased for you, but your nugget is not for me, thank you." And I turned away from my dear love, knowing that I had averted trouble, but wishing that I had the courage to walk out the door to join him.

He stood there for a long moment, as did my father, neither saying a word. Then Jem turned and walked away. Father slammed the door and turned on me.

"Young woman. If ever that fellow comes here again, if ever I hear that you have spoken to him, if ever I find that you have had any communication with him whatever, I shall have him run out of town immediately! I shall set the traps on him!"

Fine words. I prepared some of my own. If ever again my father gambles away money that rightfully belongs to his wife; if ever again my father deliberately lies to his parents-in-law, his wife and his daughter; if ever again my father comes drunk to his house and distresses his wife; if ever again my father bullies . . . I was working myself up to a fine state until I glanced across at Mama.

"Father! Help me!" Between us we carried her limp body to her bed, then I fetched some of the physic that seemed to help her. Father stood looking down at her for a while; then, with a stern glance at me, he walked out of the house. I had an uneasy certainty that he had heard every word of my thoughts!

I was certain also that I must see Jem immediately and put things to rights with him before it was too late. But I was afraid to leave my mother alone and so ill, and I knew that my father would not return from the hotel until very late. I sat in great distress at the table, tapping the edge of the clumsy candle maker and wishing most strongly that we had never come to this place.

Suddenly, and very faintly, I heard a whistle. I stopped my tapping and listened carefully. Sure enough, it was the first few bars of my beloved *Irish Washerwoman* coming from the direction of the creek. I picked up my sputtering, stinking candle and opened the front door.

I waited, and then he came.

"Ann, for you," he said. "My first nugget. Will you take it like the dear girl you are and cash it in for something you yearn for?"

"Oh, no," I whispered, moving him away from the light that came through the door just in case Father returned early. "You must buy something for yourself, or bank it. Oh Jem, I *am* so delighted for you, but we must be very careful in future. Papa will be most horribly angry if he ever sees us together."

"Then we shall take fine care that he does not."

"He has my welfare at heart . . ."

"I am sure that he has. A fine gentleman like himself, and me a worthless Irishman! How could he fancy the likes of me for his daughter! And now, Ann Bird, if you will not take the nugget, will you kindly give me back the money I left with you, and the diamond pin?"

Had I offended him so deeply that he could no longer trust me with the care of his possessions? Sadly I turned away and went to my chest where the small bundle lay. I brought it back to the door and gave it to him.

"Thank you," he said. "Now go inside to the warm and take care of your mother."

I was dismissed. I put out my hand to touch him but

he was busy stowing his precious nugget beside the rest of his hoard.

"Good-bye, Jem," I said as he tramped off toward the ford.

He did not answer, and I crept to my mother's side to watch her through the night.

Sally

"WHAT do you mean, 'separation'? You mean divorce, don't you? That's what you mean. *Divorce!*"

It's an odd thing, I know, but I had never faced up squarely to the fact that my parents might be heading for a divorce. I suppose I'd been expecting a miracle, a slick solution of the kind I'd seen on a trillion television series or read of in a million stories. There's this family and the parents are having a stormy time, and the kids all get together and cook up a plot to show the parents how they all mean so much to each other and how cutesy they are, and by the end of the half-hour or whatever it is they're all hugging and grinning as if nothing bad had ever happened to any of them.

Those scriptwriters should have sat in on some of my parents' more rabid confrontations; then they'd have realized that a smart-alec homily from a kid or the sharing of a mild family crisis is just not enough to wipe out *that* amount of bitterness. But even though I'd been there for most of them, it hadn't dawned on *me* that the situation was beyond repair. So I bawled at my mother over the telephone, when I really wanted to kick myself for being so stupid.

"When you know the full story, you might under-stand."

Typical of Ma. She had no intention of telling me the "full story" as she called it—she considered me far too young to know all the details—yet she lumbered me with her side of the problem whenever an argument came up.

"You'll tell me the full story when I come home then? You'll do that?"

"Darling, your father and I both love you very much. We definitely will not have you hurt by this, so when you come home, we'll talk things through and work out what's best for you, and that will be what's best for all of us."

I'd never heard such rubbish in my life! What would be best for me would be for them to stay together and just stop fighting. Countries can declare truces in a war, for heaven's sake. They can even fight to the death and afterward get on together and trade and everything, but a pair of grown-up people don't seem able . . .

"Okay, Ma. See you next week. Thanks for calling."

Fifteen minutes later Pa called to assure me that all he and Ma wanted was for me to be happy, and to promise that whatever happened, I wouldn't be hurt. I realized while he was saying this that it was a way of fixing their own consciences. If they got in first and said they didn't want me to be hurt, then it couldn't be their fault if I was. Hurting me wasn't part of their plan! I knew they both loved me, but they were still going to do what suited them, and if I was shattered by it, they'd expect me to refrain from mentioning the fact, because they'd prac-tically *told* me they were doing all this with my happiness in mind.

I can't remember ever being as angry as I was when I finally put the telephone down. It wasn't crying anger, more a slow-combustion rage. Three of us who lived together and knew each other pretty well had arrived at the point where we were going to split, and there didn't seem to be anything I could do about it. Mainly because the parents were taking the highly unselfish attitude that what they were doing was partly aimed at not hurting me!

Well, I had news for them. I hurt. I really hurt. I went out to the side veranda and slumped down on the old leather sofa and glared at the low line of hills that the setting sun was washing with waves of pinkness. Cooper was probably right. I shouldn't even try to take sides; better to stand back a bit and let them do what they had planned. Trouble is, it's easier to say than to do.

One of my problems was that we'd done a count in our class at school last term, and every fourth kid had parents who'd been divorced, some of them more than once. I'd felt a sort of sneaking pity for those kids, not having a stable home life, caring parents, secure emotional background, all the things you read about in the newspapers. And here I was going to be one of them, and somewhere there was some busybody creep destined to go around feeling sorry for *me*!

Aunt Bess bustled by and left a cup of tea and scones with jam, which was appreciated. She didn't say one word, either, which was appreciated even more. I didn't want the food, but I find eating a great comfort in times of stress, so I was on my third scone when Annie and Davey joined me. Annie snatched the last scone and they shared it, which I thought a bit much, because no doubt they'd been scoffing afternoon tea in the kitchen while I was suffering on the telephone in the hall.

"Ma told us. Anything we can do?"

"Now what the hell do you think *you* could do, Annie Cooper? I mean, I'm their daughter and *I* can't think of anything to do. They're separating. Pa's moved out already I think, so in a year's time from now I'll be the child of a broken marriage."

"Hey! You reckon there's . . . someone else?"

Davey did have a prurient mind on him for someone only twelve years old.

"Oh, Davey, don't be so *lewd*. You reckon there is, Sal?"

It would explain a lot of things.

"Don't know. And I don't much care. It's their lives they're messing around with, not mine." I tried very hard to mean it. "Time to do the horses, isn't it? I'll help. I don't mind, really." Tried very hard to mean that, too.

"Cooper and Dad are doing it, giving us a day off, and Ma says do you want to go to Evensong, because she'll take you if you think it'd help."

"No, *thank* you."

"Hey, Sal, I reckon it's not much help, church and all that. Hey, you know what? I've been praying for rain for six whole months now, that's about, er, twenty-four weeks, coupla hundred days of solid praying and we haven't had only that spot a coupla nights ago. See what I mean?"

I was sorry that David was losing his faith at such an early age, but I didn't have any answers to give him either, so I went to my room and had a bit of a cry, mostly for my poor parents really. I hoped there wasn't someone else, not yet at least, because I could remember when they had been so fond of each other.

I groped under my pillow, brought out the nugget brooch, and ran my finger over the inscription.

ANN

BIRD

JEM

EVER

Suddenly I realized that there were not two names on
the back of the brooch. There was no Ever family involved. Jem could be Jem Smith or Jem anything, for
all I'd know. The EVER was the promise people in love
make to each other. Like *yours eternally, forever true, always in my heart,* and all the rest of the rubbish they say.
The man who had had this brooch inscribed for his
Ann, or inscribed it himself, had to have had a short
word because he was either not a very confident in-
scriber or unable to afford to pay someone for a longer
message. EVER. It was a good word really, short and
pithy.

I was sure I was right, and I was now left with

ANN

BIRD

and JEM

Ann Bird would have to be one person, unless she was
Ann something and his pet name for her was Bird, as
in "Ann, my treasure," "mon petit choux," "my little
lamby-pie," stuff like that. But I doubted that they bothered with that kind of junk in those days. So there must
have been a family of Birds somewhere that had had an
Ann in it. Probably not even from the district anyway,
probably just happened to be passing by the home paddock one day and had dropped her stupid brooch down
the old mine shaft.

I despaired of ever solving the mystery, but actually
I was closer than I imagined.

That evening we were all sitting around, Davey and Cooper were watching some boring old replay of some boring old soccer match, Uncle James was trying to read one of the Sunday newspapers while Auntie Bess persisted in reading bits of hers out loud to him. Auntie Bess has a peculiar allergy to silence. None of us really wanted to know the weather forecast for the whole state, since there was no sign of rain in our part, nor did we yearn to hear who was who on the social scene in the city. But she read it to us anyway, and Annie and I sat with the Scrabble board between us and tried to make up dirty words with the letters. Not easy. Well, not easy to find anything *new* and dirty.

Suddenly Aunt Bess exclaimed, "Well, fancy that! Dear, I say dear, here's your cousin, well he's your nephew really isn't he, young Malcolm, and his wife and the baby. Do look, dear."

Dear mumbled, "Hmm? Hmm." Which usually satisfied Aunt Bess. The first "Hmm" has a note of interested inquiry in it, leading the listener to fancy that Uncle James understands and appreciates what is being said to him. The second "Hmm" sounds final and dismissive, as if the topic has been fully discussed and is now over and done with. But this time it didn't work.

"Very clear picture for a newspaper, they're so often all grainy, aren't they? Could be anyone. But this is definitely young Malcolm and his wife. Remember their wedding? And the baby, a gorgeous little boy, and fancy that, dear, they've called him Jem. Actually christened him Jem! Now that's a turnaround, isn't it? I mean, it isn't Jem Cooper, he's Jem Bartholomew of course, but it's interesting, isn't it? That the young ones are going back to the old names?"

It certainly was interesting. I dropped my swag of letters and dashed over to have a look at the picture. Sure enough, there was a young couple, as trendy as hell, holding a fat little baby between them, and he looked trendy too. Underneath it said, *Young Jem Bartholomew parties with parents Liz and Malcolm. Do we have another legal eagle here?*

"And do we care? Those papers talk a lot of rot! Poor kid might want to be a plumber or a vet." Annie was scornful.

"Why is it interesting that they called the baby Jem?"

"Now Annie, don't go on like that. You like Malcolm and Liz. . . ."

"Why is it interesting that they . . . ?"

"But Mum, it's so *cutesy*! 'Another legal . . . ' "

". . . and it *is* a legal sort of party, see. All the families are there to . . ."

"Why is it—"

"Hey! May we have a bit of shush here? This is a top game. Man can't hear the score, you females yakking over there!"

"Very well, Davey dear. Annie, you're disturbing the boys' game. Do go on with your Scrabble. Quietly."

She's full of surprises. I don't know what magic touch old Davey possesses, but Aunt Bess proceeded to read the paper without saying another word, and Annie meekly went back to our table. So of course I had to go too, but I now had a clue to go on with. A young relative of the Coopers had chosen to christen his son Jem, the name of my nugget person, or one of them. This had caused sufficient interest in Aunt Bess's mind to make her tell Uncle James about it.

I Scrabbled halfheartedly with Annie, promising to buy her Trivial Pursuit for next Christmas so that we'd have something different to play if ever I should come again.

Scrabble's a tad too much like a spelling lesson for my taste.

At last the stupid sports session was over and Cooper turned the television off. Before they could all dash off to bed, as this family has a habit of doing at a ridiculously early hour, I raised my voice and shouted,

"Aunt Bess! Jem!"

"Yes?"

"Yes?"

"Yes?"

I gaped as Aunt Bess, Uncle James, and Cooper all turned and answered my call!

"What?" was all I could think of to say.

"What is it, dear? Don't you feel well? James, I do think, poor child . . . It's been a very difficult day for . . . you know, Stella and George . . . Get her some hot milk please, Annie."

"I'm all right. Really. I don't need milk. It's just . . . the name Jem. You said it was interesting, and I wanted to know why it was interesting. You know, that Malcolm and that Liz called their baby . . . and then I said Jem, and Cooper and you and Uncle Jim . . ."

Then they all fell about laughing at me, of course. At last when they managed to pull themselves together, Uncle James came over and put his arm around my shoulder.

"Poor Sal. We do apologize for being so boorish, don't we Bess, kids? Didn't mean to be rude, but you sounded so funny!"

They all apologized very sweetly, and I waited. No one offered any more explanation, so I had to jump in feet first again.

"Well, can anyone tell me? Why is 'Jem' so interesting?"

Cooper grinned at me as they all drifted out through the door to their bedrooms.

"Because it's our name, stupid. Dad's and mine. We were both christened Jem. Eldest sons. See?"

Of course I didn't see a thing, and flounced off to bed too because it was obvious that no one was going to offer me any more explanations that night.

Ann

MY mother died last week. There was no nurse but me to attend her, and she was too frail at the last to stand the journey into Gulgong to see the doctor there, even if Papa could have afforded it. I did my very best, but toward the end I could see that she was almost eager to go. Since we came here, her life has been so difficult and so far from all she has ever known that she has indeed been "half in love with easeful death," and her going was as quiet and gentle as she had been herself.

Jane Prew was a great help with the funeral arrangements, and I allowed her to be. Well, the truth is that where Jane Prew is concerned, one is forced to allow! She even managed to subdue my father, who at first showed signs of wanting to take charge of affairs himself. He quickly realized that Jane Prew was capable of doing it better, and even forbore calling her his "good woman" for this once.

The butcher, Mr. Dobson, has an arrangement with a miner who was previously a carpenter by trade. Mr. Dobson keeps a supply of pine planks in a shed behind his house, and when there is a death here, he and the carpenter quietly and with admirable discretion have a coffin prepared in case the family asks for it.

So my mother lay at last in her simple box of pine, and my feelings were of grief for myself, who would miss her so much, but some gladness also for her, who was now at peace and free from pain.

I took down from the mantel the foolish length of lace that she had put there and that we had had so many arguments about. I washed and ironed it more carefully than I ever had before, and then I placed it across my mother's hands and kissed her for the last time.

Father sat in his chair brooding. "I cannot go on here much longer, Ann. With your mother gone . . . this is not the life I had envisaged for her . . . for any of us. . . . I have had the most dreadful run of luck. . . ."

Mrs. Prew, who was bustling about the room like a small clockwork doll, straightening chairs and arranging plates of food that she and Mrs. Dobson had brought, stopped and stared at him with her mouth and eyes opened to their widest.

"Luck!" she gasped. "Luck! I'd say there was them that's had worse luck than himself, and them not too far away neither. And whose fault might that be then? I ask you! Not the poor dear innocents that he's dragged all the way . . ."

Fat and beautiful Mrs. Dobson stifled her friend with one of her generously given and usually unexpected hugs, and indeed I doubt that my father was listening anyway, so engrossed was he in his own problems.

There is no graveyard at Pelican Creek, although I have heard that the squatter has begun one where a church is to be built on a corner of his land. We chose to bury my mother in the customary style, close by the house and a short distance from the old gum tree where I, and sometimes she, used to sit and sew.

Dear Mrs. Prew had arranged for a grave to be dug (strange to be calling her dear, but she has been kind and generous to me), and *dear* Mrs. Dobson had insisted that it should be dug facing east-west so that my mother's coffin might be laid facing the rising sun and in readiness for the Second Coming! She explained this to Papa and me with touching earnestness, than gave me one of her warm and warming hugs. Papa said, "Rubbish, woman!" and took my arm, probably so that I would not be touched further by those whom he considered the lower classes.

I know that funerals are sad occasions, but at first I found my mother's weirdly funny! It all seemed to be happening at some distance from me and to some other people entirely. I was deeply grateful to the two women who helped so generously, but they and my father's attitude toward them made me giggle like a madwoman, and it was extremely difficult to force my laughter to stay behind my face.

Mr. Dobson read the service. There was a small gathering, perhaps ten people, and I still felt curiously apart from it all, until I heard Mr. Dobson say, "Comfort us again now after the time that thou hast plagued us: and for the years wherein we have suffered adversity."

Then I felt the stupid, futile tears gush from my eyes, and I sobbed and sobbed for my poor little mother who had suffered such undeserved loneliness and adversity in this place.

But my father put his arm about my shoulder, and that gesture stopped my crying. I made a solemn promise at that moment that I would help my father as much as I could and serve him as well as my mother would have wished me to. But I also vowed that I would never allow him to make decisions that affected *my* life nor ever follow him without question as my poor, weak mother had done. I would find a way to support myself, to be independent of him, and so be free.

As I made my decision, I looked up, and there, just far enough away to appear separate from but almost a part of the funeral party, stood the squatter's son. My father saw him at the same time and made a low bow of gratification. I stared at the young man coldly. If he cared for my mother, he could have come right to the graveside instead of loitering at the fringe as if ashamed to be seen. I decided that he had not previously witnessed a miner's funeral and that curiosity had brought him there.

Of Jem there was no sign, but I had not seen him since the night when he had asked me to give him back his savings, so it did not surprise me that he did not choose to attend. Since that night I had also made my infrequent trips to the Chinaman's vegetable gardens by a route that went nowhere near Jem's claim, and I took care never to hum *The Irish Washerwoman* when I walked!

After the ceremony, such as it was, we went back to our hut to partake of the funeral meats the ladies had provided. I was surprised at how hungry I was, and Mistresses Prew and Dobson made sure that my plate was always full. Father came up to the table and peered closely at the platters of cold roast beef and mutton, fresh bread and the delicate pastries my mother used to love, made with such care by the baker and his wife. He moved some of the meats about on their plates with the end of a serving fork, then shook his head and walked away, as if the food was not good enough for his palate.

I quickly swallowed the forkful of beef I was chewing, stepped forward, and spoke loudly.

"My father and I wish to thank you all for coming today to see my dear mother to her rest. We also wish to thank you for your kind generosity in providing this lavish and elegant repast." It sounded somewhat flowery when I said it, but it pleased all of the mourners, and *dis*pleased my father greatly, so I was content.

Later that evening, when we were alone, my father said, "We shall not be staying here very much longer,

100 A NUGGET OF GOLD

Ann. That mine will never provide a decent living, let alone a fortune. I shall look into the possibility of leasing a sheep property, perhaps farther west. Even Queensland has possibilities, I hear."

I made my first move toward acting upon what I had decided that afternoon. "You may go as soon as you please, Father, but I shall not be leaving here."

I think it may have been the very first time that anyone, or at least any woman, had argued with Papa!

"I beg your pardon?"

"I think you heard me, Papa. I am beginning to make some friends here." (Although I feared I had lost the one I desired most.)

"Friends indeed, miss! You mean the wives of the local tradesmen, no doubt. The women who were here today. A young lady of your education and background is deserving of better than this. No, I promised your mother I would take care of you, and I shall do that by removing you from this uncivilized place. We may even return to England. How would you like that, eh?"

"My mother would have loved to return," I answered coldly, "but I think we should face the fact that we have not the money for our fares. Not, so far as I know, for both of us."

He looked away when I said that, and I began to suspect that he did indeed have money concealed somewhere, money that he had kept back, knowing full well how much Mother and I had to scrimp on what he gave us to keep house.

I wanted no further conversation with him and was pleased to hear a knocking at the door.

"Blast!" Father exploded, thinking it was another of my "tradesman friends" come calling. But it was the squatter's son again, and although I welcomed a visitor to curtail the talk with my father, I wished it could have been other than he. Father pulled him inside and thrust him down in the best chair, then fluttered around him like a moth mesmerised by a flame.

"So kind . . . pay your respects . . . beloved wife . . . very simple service . . . not what one would have . . . strange country . . . away from one's own kind . . . forgive daughter's silence. . . . heartbroken. . . . *you* would understand . . ."

I sat by the table, determined to say not one word, to allow my father to impress the young man as much as he could.

Charles seemed ill at ease and glanced frequently in my direction as if seeking help, but I gave him none. At last he was able to break in on my father's fawning chatter.

"I came, sir, to offer my condolences to you and to your daughter." He nodded in my direction and I still said not one word. He continued to look directly at me as he went on, "If there is anything at all I can do to assist you . . ."

"Oh, upon my word, how kind, how well expressed, my dear young man. But I do assure you, no assistance is necessary. No, no, no, we are quite well situated, although . . . for the moment . . . man of the world . . . you would understand."

It was quite obvious to me that Charles did not understand one word of this, but I let them go on.

"The . . . er, grave, sir. You intend to leave it . . . er?"

"Well, a gravestone out here does seem to be somewhat out of place, don't you think?" So my mother was to be denied a gravestone as well! "On the other hand, I believe it is the custom to plant a tree, some sort of marker . . ."

"I do like a gravestone myself, sir, but then again, a tree is a very pleasant reminder. . . ."

"My wife was a lover of nature, sir. Man-made edifices did not please her so well."

My mother enjoyed *gardens*, to be sure, so long as they were tended by someone other than herself. But she *greatly* admired "man-made edifices" and would willingly have done without bread for herself to put a tablet to his memory on my *father's* grave.

I seethed as they went on.

"In that case, sir, I imagine a tree of some sort would do very well."

"Ye-es. But hardly one of these ugly natives, I think. You do agree, I am sure. An English lady would prefer an English tree."

"Of course."

I was beginning to feel some sympathy for the poor young man, in spite of my dislike.

"Unfortunately English trees are very hard to come by in this remote area of the Empire." There was a long and heavy pause. "But no doubt I could order one. . . . It may take some time of course . . . a longer time than I may be vouchsafed perhaps. . . ."

"Oh, no. Do allow me. We have elm trees in my mother's garden. Do permit me to bring you a sapling to plant here."

"No, no, my dear fellow, I could not allow that at all."

"My mother would be most willing to let you have one, I know."

I also knew that his poor mother must be heartily tired of losing eggs, candle-makers, and now elm trees to people whom she had not even met! But I said nothing.

Charles stood up. "I must go now, but I shall return with a sapling as soon as I can. . . . When Mother is . . . very shortly. I promise."

I gave him a very cool bow as he left and quickly retired to my bed so that Father was unable either to resume his conversation regarding our future or to gloat over the patronage of the squire's son.

The following day Charles arrived with a healthy elm sapling bundled in a sack with plenty of rich earth around its roots. Father had stayed at home, reluctant to resume his work at the mine; eager to be seen as mourning his wife, no doubt. He insisted that I accompany them to the grave, and we stood together while Charles dug a hole in the hard earth and planted the tree for us.

I had to admit that it was a very kindly act, and I thanked him for it when he was done. He did not linger this time; all Father had to do was to invite him inside to take tea with us and he was reminded of a hundred chores he had promised to do for his family!

"I hope that I may call again, sir?" he said as he was leaving, and my father assured him of a welcome at any time. I gave him no such assurance, but bade him a civil farewell and hurried off to check the water level in the butt by the old tree stump.

Sally

THE Cooper family must be the most laconic lot in the world, with the exception of Aunt Bess, who could take an Olympic gold medal for talking, and that's competing against any country you can name! But the rest of them make you scramble for every tiny bit of information you want, and never offer a word of help.

Take Cooper, for instance. I mean there he is, christened Jem, lets everybody call him Cooper. Cooper Cooper for crying out loud! They must have laughed their heads off at him when he was at school, and I don't suppose it bothered him one little bit. All my life I've called him Cooper, and of course it never occurred to him to say, "My real name's Jem, but they call me Cooper for some reason or other." Oh no, that might be telling someone something that person wanted to know. Giving away a bit of information that might be useful to someone!

And they all have a habit of ignoring a person. At breakfast the morning after the Jem business, I frantically tried to work the conversation around to names, and all they wanted to talk about was what they'd all be doing that day and which form of transport each of them would be using. Uncle James, whom I could *not* think of as a

"Jem," was taking some stock to the sales with a neighbor first thing. They all looked serious when this was discussed, so I guessed the prices were down again and it was a job he'd prefer not to be doing.

Annie and Cooper were going to search for a bull that had gone missing. On horseback, so it wasn't even suggested that I should give them a hand. I was still getting accustomed to standing in the same yard as a horse without gibbering with fear, so the suggestion that I should board one and let it prance about with me clinging to its neck had not been made. Particularly not by me.

Aunt Bess said she had a meeting of the Country Women's Association to go to and was hoping to visit a friend in hospital after that, so she'd be using the station wagon and would take a load of garbage to the town dump on the way, and would I like to go with her, Sally dear?

Sally dear thought not, thanks. I had a feeling that a meeting of the CWA, although uplifting and worthy and all that, might just lack a touch of sparkle for me, a visit to the friend in hospital would only depress, and the thought of traveling in the station wagon loaded to the Plimsoll line with bags of household garbage failed to fill me with enthusiasm either!

"Hey, Sal. You'll like it at the dump, honest. I found a perfectly good train set there once when I was a kid, and there's been lawnmowers and motors and stuff. Mum might even let *you* bring some of it home."

I perceived the scars of many old wounds in Davey's words. Visions of a treasure trove that he had been forced to abandon because of parental fastidiousness. Motors and stuff that dreams are made on!

"Don't you have a regular garbage collection?" I stupidly inquired.

Gave them all a laugh. I certainly was paying my way in amusement value.

"Out here?"

"You crazy, Sal?"

"The boys usually bury it, dear. Dig pits out the back there. . . ."

"A regular garbage collection! Hey, that's a good one!"

". . . with the drought the ground's too hard . . ."

"It's a temporary arrangement; the shire council permits it."

"She's too proud to travel with the garbage bags, aren't you, Sal?"

"I'll go with you, Ma. On condition I get to bring just one thing home. Right?"

Aunt Bess ignored Davey and turned to me. "You're very welcome to come, dear. I thought it might be a pleasant change for you to come into town for a few hours. Of course, you don't have to do anything about the garbage. They're teasing you. Stop teasing her, children. And David, I will not have you at the dump ever again, thank you. I promised myself that about four years ago, the time you found all those grubby plastic cups and wanted to bring them home to be washed and used again."

"Well, it's wasteful, innit? I mean, all those perfectly good cups, and brand new practically."

"Oh, Davey! Yuk, yuk, yuk!"

"I bet some of them hadn't been used at all!"

"David, I want you to come with me to the sales. It's time you got some experience."

Clever Uncle James. Davey sped off to get ready, the treasures of the dump forgotten already. That left me still unprovided for. I thought fast. They were so kind that if I suggested just staying at home by myself they'd worry about me, and anyway the thought of doing nothing at all with one's time was obviously anathema to the Cooper family of movers and doers.

"I thought I might walk over and visit Mr. Cooper, if

that would be all right," I said. "After I've done my share of the work, of course."

Groans and scoffing noises from my best friend Annie, but Aunt Bess and Uncle James were very pleased, and she telephoned Grandpa Cooper to make sure he'd look out for me later in the morning.

I saw them all off to their diverse pursuits, then set off to walk to the big homestead. Down the hill to the creek first, but without calling at the mine shaft this time. I don't know why, but I felt I'd prefer to have someone with me when I visited that hole again. Even the company of the Cooper kids was better than looking into its grim blackness alone. I know it wasn't all that deep, but it certainly wasn't the most cheerful place I'd ever been in.

I paused for a moment by the willows at the ford, but didn't cross it, because Pelican is on the same side of the creek as Hillside. It wasn't far, but the day was hot so I was mightily relieved when the house came into sight.

I'd seen it only by night when we went to the woolshed dance, and it looked beautiful then, but now, in daylight, it was superb!

I think they call the style Georgian. It was made of stone, with a sandstone veranda along the front and around the sides and tall, fluted columns holding up the veranda roof. There was a big double front door with a glass fanlight above and two French doors on each side of it, with shutters. Upstairs there were five windows along the front and two chimneys on each side. The fence had a white hawthorn hedge clipped level with it, and there were lots of enormous trees in the garden, pines and elms and what I thought might be an oak tree. It was a really splendid house, and as I stood looking at it, the front door opened and Mr. Cooper came out to meet me.

There was a central hallway leading from the front door to another door at the back, and he led me through there and into a sort of courtyard with verandas around the sides and an old well in the center. The kitchen was an enormous room taking up one side of the courtyard, and he took me in there to meet his housekeeper, Mrs. Dobson.

And I was lucky to spot her, I can tell you. Mrs. Dobson must be the thinnest, smallest, lightest person I've ever met. She came up to about my shoulder, and her dress had to be reefed in at the waist with a wide belt to keep it from trailing on the floor. She wore little-girl shoes that I suppose were the only ones she could get that would fit her snidgy little feet. Her hair was sparse, but heavily corrugated and bright orange in color. It matched her lipstick exactly and was only a shade darker than the rouge that glowed on each cheek.

"Well, you'll know me next time, love, won't you? I say, she'll know me next time, Mr. Cooper."

I was so embarrassed, I was tempted to lunge across, seize the big knife she was holding and stab myself terminally in the stomach. Luckily I didn't do that straight away, because I saw in a second that they were both laughing fit to bust, and she didn't seem the least bit offended that I'd been staring at her so rudely.

"Well, Mrs. Dobson, I don't suppose the poor girl's ever seen the likes of you before. And never likely to again, either! You're a once-in-a-lifetime experience; I've often told you that."

She seemed tickled to death at this doubtful compliment and put down her knife to shake my hand. I took hers carefully in mine so as not to crush it to pieces and had four fingers mangled in a grip that made my eyeballs pop. For a lady her size she certainly had an impressive clutch!

"Pleased to meet you, love. Sit down, why don't you?"

Why indeed? The thing was that I was so weak from her handshake that I could barely stand, so I sank down on one of the old Windsor chairs that were set around the table, and gently massaged my throbbing fingers on my lap out of sight. But they both knew what I was doing, and I had to give them that one. I'd been rude to stare and I'd been punished in a manner of speaking, so we were now even, and Mrs. Dobson was obviously not bearing a grudge.

"I'm sorry I stared at you, Mrs. Dobson," I gasped through the pain. I was going to say that I'd been admiring her dress, or her hair or something, but decided that she was going to see through any weak excuse I could make. This old lady was no fool. "It's just that you're the . . . slimmest person I've ever met, and for a fatty like me that's interesting. I'm very glad to meet you though."

"That's all right, love. I'm used to people staring at me. Doesn't bother me none. Anyway, who says you're a fatty? Nicely set up you are. Very nicely set up. Now, how about you do the grand tour with Mr. Cooper there while I make us all a nice cup of tea?"

So we did the grand tour, and grand it was. All the doors and skirting boards and fireplaces were made of cedar, and so was the great staircase that took us to the bedrooms above. Mr. Cooper had to tell me that (about the cedar); to me it was just a highly polished, warm sort of reddish wood. Beautiful, though; it suited the house very well.

The Pelican homestead made every other house I'd been in seem poky by comparison. The ceilings were high, the walls were thick, the floors were polished wood, cedar too for all I'd know (Mr. Cooper didn't specify), with Persian carpets on them—and talk about furniture!

I've seen antique *markets* in the city with less stock in them than this place had. There were collections of plates in glass-fronted cabinets, old paintings on the walls, and on the mantels and tables were vases of fresh flowers and groups of family photographs in beautiful silver frames. No wonder Mrs. Dobson was so skinny with all that to keep clean and dusted.

There were two kitchens, one they called the scullery, with enormous sinks made of terrazzo, as old-fashioned as anything, along one wall, and enormous freezers made of stainless steel, as modern as ditto, along another.

"A bit grand for just the two of us, isn't it?" Mr. Cooper laughed. "But we installed big freezer units when the children were young, and it seemed a good idea to keep them on. This way we can stock up for both Hillside and Four Mile. More room to spare here, you see. And eventually, when I go, young Cooper will move in here, with a wife and family I hope, so the old place should be kept in going order for the next generation. Always been the thing here, you see. Eldest son takes over the big house. James should have, of course, but he preferred to stay on at Hillside. . . ."

"That's great, Mr. Cooper, but could you tell me—"

"Tea's up!" Mrs. Dobson beckoned us back into the main kitchen, where one end of the long table had been set with loaded plates enough to stock the food hall of a large department store. I had a quick peep at my watch; too early for lunch, so this must be morning tea!

"Come along now, tuck in. Do you good. Pass this to Mr. Cooper would you, dear, and cut him a slice of that cherry cake to have after his scone."

We tucked in, and she was right, it did do me good. And to my surprise Mrs. Dobson ate as much as I did. I do think it's unfair the way some people can do that. I mean, the skinniest people I know at school are the ones who binge on just about everything that's bad for them, and they never put on a pound, while I eat like a sparrow most of the time, well some of the time then, and I'm always overweight. I think I may study biology or whatever when I leave school, to find out why that is so. It's the sort of research that could lead to a Nobel prize, I reckon.

Mrs. Dobson's beady eye caught me staring again, so she explained that she came from a long line of cooks and bakers, and she figured that because she'd been around it all her life, food didn't have the same effect on her that it did on some people. I may include that theory in my future studies.

"You'd be interested in that, Sally," Mr. Cooper said while grappling with the hefty slice of apple shortcake that was following the cherry cake and the scone. "Mrs. Dobson's family lived in the township we were speaking of the other night. The gold-mining settlement they called Pelican Creek. It *was* you I was talking to, wasn't it?"

At last! We were on to history and I could get some answers.

"Yes, Mr. Cooper, we were talking about it, and I wanted to ask you why . . ."

"Too right they did," Mrs. Dobson cut in. "My great-grandfather was the baker in Pelican Creek. I well remember my granny telling about the early days. . . ."

". . . the boys were christened . . ." I soldiered on.

"Not many of them, I can tell you that. On account of there was no church, nothing but a traveling priest or minister now and then, so christening wasn't taken for granted, the way it is now. Not that everyone cares so much these days. . . ."

I thought she'd never stop! A knock-out match between Aunt Bess and Mrs. Dobson would be something to see. Hear.

"I *know*, Mrs. Dobson. I *know* what you mean, but

some of the boys around here were christened Jem, weren't they, Mr. Cooper? Why is that, do you know?" My old tried-and-true method of rerouting my maternal grandfather's conversations, and it worked again.

"I should think I do know, young Sally," Mr. Cooper laughed. "I'm one of them, aren't I?"

Suddenly I felt surrounded by Jems. I'd really only needed one.

"Yes. I was christened Jem. I was the oldest boy, you see, and all the oldest boys in the Cooper family are automatically christened Jem. Simple really."

Not simple really. But he went on without prompting, and Mrs. Dobson was busily helping herself to more grub.

"Hasn't been popular, mind you. Not among the oldest boys anyway. All very well early on; in those days Jem was quite a common name, and I didn't mind myself. Although I did get a bit of ribbing when I was younger. But people get accustomed to names, you know. I expect you could call a fellow just about any old name, and if he was a reasonably decent chap people wouldn't think too much about it. Tried to tell my young Jem that, but of course he was born during the war, and by the time I'd come back, his mother had them all calling him James, so I really couldn't upset the apple cart by insisting, now could I?"

I realized *that* Jem was Uncle James.

"And of course I didn't have any say at all when young Cooper came along. He was *christened* Jem of course, no problem about that. We like a bit of family tradition in the country, you know, but there was no question of *calling* him that. Mind you, I think I'd have chosen something a bit better than Cooper. Seems odd to me. Cooper Cooper. Still, that's the way it goes. . . ."

"And speaking of going. Off you go, my friend. I'll

call you in good time for your dinner." Mrs. Dobson turned to me. "He always has a nap this time of day. Doctor's orders. A little nap before his meal." (Before his meal! What that old gentleman had just put away would be enough for most people for a week, and she was already planning his next binge! What a jewel of a housekeeper to have.) "Does him the world of good. Come along now, Mr. Cooper." And the bossy little biddy shooed him off to bed before I could explore my Jems any further.

I stacked the dishes while she put away the small amount of food that was left over. She wouldn't let me stay and help with the washing up; I had to let her shoo me out just as she'd done to him.

But she said I was welcome to come again anytime, and as I trotted back down to the creek, full of delicious food and with some more information, but not enough, about Jem, and glowing from the beauty of the old home-stead, I felt the visit had been well worthwhile.

Ann

I bake a very dull damper. As a matter of fact *everything* I bake is dull and so lacking in flavor that it surprises me how many flies gather to devour it the moment I put it on the table! They swarm through the windows, jostle each other to come in through the door, and settle in black, buzzing clouds upon my poor efforts before I can put a cover in place. I suppose I should be pleased to see such appreciation for my indifferent cooking. Father eats what I put before him and never comments on it. I think he refuses to see the flies in case he is expected to do something about them, but I am determined to win the battle against the filthy creatures.

To this end I raided my mother's cabin trunk and found a more profitable mine than the one my father is working. There was a voluminous petticoat of white cotton lavishly trimmed with lace insertion. There was also a set of whalebone stays, a long, inflexible harness far too rigid for my liking, which I quickly stuffed down into the bottom of the trunk, and gowns of muslin and tarlatan, moiré and silk, much too grand for wearing here. My poor mama, what dreams she had.

No doubt when my own garments are completely

threadbare I shall be forced to lengthen them to wear myself, but I replaced them for the moment. Until I can afford the ten pounds to purchase one of the new sewing machines I saw in Sydney, I am reluctant to make over any clothes for myself.

I also replaced the slim bundle of letters lying in the bottom of the trunk. Someday I shall have to destroy them, I suppose, but it seems too soon yet. I wish I had known of their existence sooner; then I could have put them in the coffin to accompany my mother to her grave.

I kept out the petticoat and made the very best use of it. With careful cutting and stitching I was able to make curtains for all the windows, and as I hammered them in place I rejoiced to think of the brigades and battalions of flies that would be turned away because of my efforts. My only regret was that I had not thought of this solution while Mother was alive so that she might have been relieved of one at least of her irritations. But, being Mama, she might have been reluctant to allow me to use her precious undergarments in this way.

Father did not notice the addition to our furnishings, and I was mightily pleased. I am sure that had he known that the curtains had originally been a lady's unmentionable, he would have ordered me to take them down, flies or no flies.

One day I decided to take a vacation from damper-making, so I walked down to the baker's shop to buy bread. Mrs. Prew served me with her bonnet askew and her face red and angry.

"That Prew!" she muttered. "He'll be the death of me, I swear it! 'Nice day, Jane,' he says. 'I think the fish might be biting down the far waterhole,' he says. So, baking over, off he goes and takes the children with him. 'A family outing,' he says. Some family outing! Here I am stuck in the shop serving them that fancies coming in at any time of the day that suits them, pardon me, no offense, to pay tuppence for a loaf of bread, and there they all be, down at the waterhole, having their family outing without me. Anything else you want, dearie?"

I really felt that I should spend more money after that lecture, but I had none, so to placate the angry little woman, I suggested that she should join her family for their outing and I would mind her shop for an hour or two. And should my father happen to pass by and see me serving in a bakery, I would just have to hurl myself into the great oven out the back.

"Well, I must say, that *is* civil of you, love. They went way past your hut, down the far gully there."

I had heard what I thought was a great stampede of wild and noisy buffalo accompanied by a flight of excited, chattering jackdaws when I was adjusting my curtains that morning—the Prew family no doubt, setting off on their excursion!

Mrs. Prew took off her apron and tied it on me. I felt, and looked, as if I was wearing a doll's pinafore. She tweaked my shawl straight with her tiny hand, and then she beamed and said, "Now you just wait there, dearie. I'll not be promising anything, mind, but certainly it's time something pleasant . . . Well, 'nuff said, poor child. . . ."

Then she bobbed and beamed herself out through the door, leaving me in high hopes of a fresh fish for dinner that night but wondering why she needed to be so mysterious about it.

I neatened the already neat rows of loaves on the shelf by the window, then perched on Mrs. Prew's stool with my knees up near my chin, so low it was, and breathed in the yeasty smell of the bread and pondered on the scarcity of flies in comparison with my own kitchen. The doorway here was not made of wood as ours was but consisted of a strip of sacking that did not open as wide as a door; the window was of glass, a rare luxury in Pelican Creek, so none of the little demons could enter there. I did envy Mrs. Prew her lack of flies.

It was late in the day for customers, so I took the opportunity to daydream a little. I knew it would not be long before my father moved on. He had been so restless at home in Bloomsbury that Mother had gladly fallen in with his plans to emigrate. When we arrived in Sydney after the stormy days and rolling nights at sea, *I* hoped we could settle there. But no. My grandparents' allowance was sufficient to buy a property in the country where the gentry were settled, so it was to Bathurst Father went in the fine carriage he had bought. But to Father money was like feathers to the wind, something to be played with and scattered about with no thought to the future. He was showing all the signs of his restlessness now, talking of moving on as soon as news came of the *next* gold strike, wherever it might occur, so that he would be one of the earliest arrivals. I do not know what difference that would make to his success. It seemed to me that, whatever we did, our future was bleak.

Then I sniffed again the rich and lively smell of the bakery and decided to turn my mind to another subject. But *that* offered an even more bleak future for me. I had not seen Jem for such a long time. I dared not go by his mine for fear of my father's wrath, and it seemed that he was also avoiding me. I was sure he would not have asked me to return his possessions unless he had decided to have nothing more to do with me. I decided that it was a very good thing he had done so. He was certainly not the sort of person I wished to have as a friend. His temper was too unreliable for my liking. He was ill-mannered, overbearing, and impatient, and I wanted nothing more to do with him.

The hessian at the doorway parted, and in he walked! I quickly slid my feet from the rung of the stool and almost landed on the flat of my back.

"May I help you, sir?" I asked with cold politeness.

He stood for a long while beside the rough counter, looking at me, not saying a word.

"Have you come to buy bread?" I insisted, to jog him into speech.

He glared at me impatiently. "No, I have not come to buy bread," he mimicked, "And yes, you may help me. If you've a mind to, that is. Have you a mind to, Ann Bird?"

I did not enjoy being questioned so directly and needed more time and more details of his request, so I answered, "I have a mind to help you purchase some bread. I have a mind to help you if you are in dire need of assistance. But other than that, I think I have no mind to help you at all."

He could always weaken me with a smile. He smiled his blue and black and golden smile, and I was hard put to keep my face from melting in the warmth of it.

"Come along, Ann Bird. I love that name, do you know that?"

"I wonder that you even remember my name, sir, it is so long since we met."

"I spent a few days in Gulgong, and as well as that, I had no desire to cause you trouble with your father."

"How did you know that I was here today?"

"I have many good friends, Ann Bird."

Including the baker's wife! I understood then what Mrs. Prew had been hinting at as she left me. She must have run down the hill, across the ford, and up the other side to Jem's mine to tell him that I was alone in the shop and my father not in sight. What impudence! Dear Mrs. Prew.

"I doubt I can help you, sir. But what is it you want?"

No one can know how fiercely I was hoping that he would ask me to leap upon a horse and elope with him! Me! Who finds the smallest pony a monster to be feared—and I taller than most horses I have met. Yet I would gladly have taken the risk of being thrown that day.

"Tomorrow Mr. Prew takes his dray to Gulgong for supplies. I have some business to transact there. Listen to that, Ann Bird. I have business to transact! And I want you to come with me. Mrs. Prew promises there is room for you on the dray and one of the miners has a horse he lends me to ride. Will you come?"

While elopement would have seemed quite a reasonable request, a trip to Gulgong seemed far too great an undertaking to think of.

"I cannot . . . My father . . . How long? No, I cannot . . ."

"Two hours or so there, two hours or so back. Just as long as it takes Mr. Prew. Not long. I promise. We leave straight after your father goes to his mine, after breakfast. We are back long before he returns for his evening meal. Will you come?"

"No . . . I cannot . . . He comes home for luncheon . . . No, it is quite impossible. . . . No."

"Oh, Ann! One meal! Surely we can think up an excuse for one meal! Look, girl. In the usual run of things I would never suggest that you deceive your father, but this is different. It is of great importance."

"What is?"

"I'll not tell you what it is, but it *is* of great, *great* importance. You are a clever girl. You can read and write. You must be able to think of a likely lie to be telling him."

"I cannot lie to my father!" But as I said it, I knew

that I would. "You promise to have me back before dark?"

"Promise! Good girl! Be here, in the morning, whatever time you can get away, and we'll set off then." He reached across the counter and touched my arm. "I will take care of you, Ann Bird. I swear I will."

He went to the doorway, pulled back the hessian and peered out. "No one coming," he assured me, then came back to where I was standing, already working on the story I would tell Father.

"I am truly sorry about your mother," he said. "I was away in Gulgong when she died. They told me when I came back, and I was smitten with sadness for you." (As I was smitten with love for him.) "She was a gentle lady, as you are yourself, Ann Bird, and 'tis a grievous loss, I know. I would have come to her funeral, in spite of himself, had I not been away."

I could feel the tears that I had found such difficulty in shedding, prickling now behind my eyes, so I nodded and smiled him out of the door.

The Prew family bellowed and stamped their way down the path soon afterward, and Mr. Prew, who had obviously been primed by his wife, nodded and nudged his approval for the next day's illicit arrangements. He was not one for conversation; I imagine he had long since given up trying to compete with his wife in that area.

Pretending disinterest, I assured him that I just *might* decide to come, then again I might not, and they must leave without me had I not arrived by a reasonable hour. He grinned at me from under his bushy eyebrows, and I knew I had not fooled Mr. Prew.

I then asked Mrs. Prew how she managed to keep her place so free of flies, although at that moment I should not have minded if a great swarm of the things had come to carry off the whole settlement, just as long as they left Jem and me alone. But Mrs. Prew took my query very seriously and said that she left a mixture of a half teaspoon of black pepper, one teaspoon of brown sugar, and a tablespoon of cream on a plate. She also offered a deterrent to fleas and mosquitoes, but I decided not to use that one.

"It don't smell too bad at all, love," she protested. "My little ones love the smell of it. Puts 'em to sleep a treat, it does. Honest!"

I thanked her heartily and said it sounded a marvelous idea, but I think she knew that I would put up with a million fleas and an army of mosquitoes before I would throw a pat of dried cow dung on the fire before going to bed at night.

I took my loaf and hurried home, concentrating hard on the story I would fudge for Papa and wondering at the back of my mind what important business Jem was planning to transact in Gulgong the next day.

Sally

ANNIE and Cooper were still out searching for the missing bull, so while preparing lunch for the three of us, I got down to some serious thinking about the brooch.

Now that I knew Jem was a Cooper family name, it was reasonable to suppose that the Jem on the brooch was a Cooper. If I'd known in advance that old Mr. Cooper spent just about all his daylight hours taking naps, when he wasn't eating Mrs. Dobson's feasts, I would have started questioning him earlier in my visit. As it was, I hadn't learned much at all and my time was running out fast.

So I was ready for them when they finally came clomping in, glowing and aggressive from all the riding and rounding up they'd been doing. But they, of course, weren't ready for *me*. Oh, no. The radio had to be switched on first so that we could all listen to the Country Hour while we ate, and not a word was spoken until we knew the river heights (low), the weather forecasts (no rain), the stock market report (gloomy), the price of fruit and vegetables at the markets (not good enough), the price of livestock at the sales (not anywhere *near* good enough), and finally the world news, which they were quite happy to ignore now that they knew about the really important items in their world. I do admit that the lack of rain was beginning to worry me, too. The skimpy few drops we'd had one night, which gummed up the horse paddocks and clagged the track to the sheds, were all there had been since I arrived, and each morning of clear skies cast a miserable gloom over the breakfast table, I can tell you.

But while they listened to their sad prospects being read over the airwaves, I served up the cold meat and salad, cleared the dishes, fetched the rest of last night's apricot pie and the jug of cream, and started the kettle off for tea. Then I sat opposite Cooper and fixed him with my beady eye, so that as soon as they were ready to switch off the radio, I was ready to begin.

"Okay now, Cooper. I want to know some local history. First up, which Jem Cooper struck gold around here?"

"None of them. Never into gold, the Coopers. The family was here long before the gold rush, but farming, not digging."

"Rotten squatters they were. Grabbed miles of land and the poor miners starved to death, some of them."

"Okay, Annie, let's not argue till we know something about the subject, eh?" Cooper *was* protective of his local history.

"Maybe one of them just found a nugget then. Just the one?"

"Not that I know of."

I suppose if I'd had any sense, I would have brought the stupid brooch out and showed them, but I really somehow wanted to keep it secret. In a way the feeling was connected with my worries about Ma and Pa. Everyone knew what was going on there now, and I hated having them feeling sorry for me, so the brooch was something I could work on alone, and feel that I was in control of. I wasn't, of course. The whole thing was beyond me. Maybe *this* Jem hadn't actually found the nugget. Maybe he'd bought it at the local jewelry shop and given it to his girlfriend . . . maybe last Christmas! I don't know why I had to put such historical significance on the thing. But it *was* old!

"Anyway, can't sit here talking all day." Cooper carried his plates into the kitchen and set off toward the back door. "Dad said I had to cover that shaft you tumbled down the other night, so I'd better do it now, before young Davey comes back and wants to help."

"Pity about the stone," Annie murmured as she carried *her* dishes out for me to wash.

Suddenly I was alert. I sensed there was something of more significance coming, and I recalled the feeling of smoothish stone beneath me at the bottom of the pit.

"What stone?" I followed Cooper to the back door and held it closed until he answered me. "What stone, Cooper?"

"The stone that was covering it. Been there as long as anyone around here can remember. We figure it was put there in the seventies."

"Cooper! That's only about ten years. What sort of memories are we talking about here?"

"*Eighteen* seventies, dope. When the gold rush was on."

He was stronger than me, so he had the door open with no trouble at all. Annie from the kitchen had to put in her two cents' worth.

"Why so interested in an old shaft, anyway?"

"Well, it's *my* shaft practically, isn't it? I mean, I was the one that fell down it. I might have *died* down there. Of course it's interesting to me. Tell me about it, Annie. You can wash if you like."

That was a worthwhile bribe. Annie hated drying the dishes, and we all hated her doing them too, because she whined the entire time about having to put them away and usually ended up shoving plates and cups just wherever she found a space, so that we sometimes hunted for utensils for days after she'd been drying. Not that I'm so much neater myself, but when it comes to eating, and that includes articles to eat with, I *care*!

"It's been there forever. Well, all my life anyway. They say it was one of the old shafts put down by the miners at the time of the gold rush, and that was eighteen seventy-something around here. Take them from the back, why don't you? Damn things dripping all over the place!"

"You said it was a pity about the lid."

"What lid? Do the plates! The *plates*!"

Honestly, I've never known anyone who can extract more drama out of doing dishes than Annie.

"The lid of the mine shaft, the stone that must have fallen into the hole before I did. That lid. Listen, why don't you let me do the lot. I don't mind washing *and* drying. *And* putting away." I quickly added the last bit in case we lost more crockery to Annie's careless impulses. "You just sit down and tell me about the stone and all that. I'm interested. I really am."

She was quick to accept. "You're peculiar, Sal, you know that? I mean, being interested in an old hole in the ground. I've lived here all my life and *I'm* not interested in it. Never have been. I guess having old Cooper rambling on about local history all the time sort of puts you off. All I know is, it's an old mine, there's lots of them about here, but this one had a special lid over the top, a sort of rounded flat stone, cracked of course, and there must have been enough rain over the past few years to make the hole bigger, or the earth to subside, or something technical like that, so that the lid finally broke and fell down the hole. Then you came bumbling along, mad as a snake, not looking where you were going. . . ."

"Well, you can hardly blame me. It was pitch-dark. . . . I wasn't bumbling. . . ."

"But you *were* mad, weren't you? As a snake. Because you'd been going on about farmers having it easy and Cooper and Davey had argued with you."

"So had you, as I recall. Anyway, that's over now. I take it all back. The farmer's life is not a happy one. The lid?"

"Yes, well, the stone must have busted and slid down into the shaft. Recently. Pa said it was there a couple of weeks ago. Actually it wouldn't matter if it didn't have a lid. We all know it's there, and there aren't any animals in the home paddock. It was just that you had to go and fall in. . . ."

"Well, I'm sorry, I'm sure! But how do you know the stone's been in place since eighteen seventy-something? I mean, it could have been put there, say, just before you were born, couldn't it?"

I'd at last finished the washing up and the wiping up and the putting away, so I draped the damp tea towels over the oven handle of the Aga and selected an apple to finish up with.

"It could have, I guess, but that would make it look a bit stupid, wouldn't it?"

I paused in my apple polishing. "Make what look a bit stupid?"

"The carving."

I wished I had something more threatening in my hand than a stupid apple. Annie needed to be straightened out, but I gritted my teeth and politely inquired, "Which—carving—Annie?"

"On the stone, ninny. I thought that was what we

were talking about. The stone that was on top of the mine shaft that you chose to loiter in, the night after you arrived here. That stone. There was carving on it. Still is, I guess."

I took one short, but heavy step toward her. "What does the carving say, Annie?"

She smiled as a tigress must smile when the mood takes her and asked, "Why, Sal? What makes you so interested in a grotty old mine shaft and an old broken stone? Hmm?"

I decided that the best thing would be to be perfectly frank with Annie. I was her guest, I owed it to her to be honest and to have no secrets from her.

"Actually, Annie, to tell you the truth, hearing Cooper talking about that old mining settlement the other day . . . well . . . I don't know, it just made me think that we all ought to know a bit more about what went on here then. It *is* our history, you know."

"Oh yeah?"

"Oh come on, Annie. It wouldn't hurt you to tell me. What did it say on the stone?"

She mimicked my voice exactly when she said: "*Actually*, Sally, to tell you the truth . . . I don't remember!"

And she was quite adamant. Wouldn't even talk about it to me again, and strode out the door in her ridiculous jodhpurs and riding boots and the big Akubra hat as if she owned the place.

I took my apple outside and walked down to the creek, across the ford, and up the opposite hill until I came to the big old gum tree with the elm nearby. I lay on the scruffy yellow grass and pondered, first on the mine shaft. Presuming the lid had been put on about a hundred years ago, when the gold mining stopped, then the brooch had been lost down the shaft more than a hundred years ago, *before* the lid was put on. Therefore, the Jem Cooper who had given the brooch to Ann Bird had lived at least a hundred years ago. I didn't think it really mattered what was carved on the stone; the brooch had been lost down there, and that was that. My problem was, which of the Jem Coopers was involved with someone called Ann Bird?

I lay there thinking for a while, then realized that of course my preoccupation with the brooch was a handy way of avoiding something that I would have to face some time. Namely, the split up of my family. I remembered what Davey had suggested, and thought of my father with another woman. At least I *tried*. Probably his secretary. But Miss Miller was such a dill! I'd met her at parties when all the partners of Pa's firm got together and pretended they were buddies, and their families were buddies and their staff were buddies. Painful memories, because I didn't feel that I was buddies with any of them. All the other kids were older and went to different schools from me, and Pa was a pretty junior partner. All the older partners went to special trouble to make us feel at home, calling Ma "m'dear" and telling her how successful Pa was, and their wives were all falling over each other to tell her how *clever* she was to have a career as well as bringing up a child and "making a home" for Pa, and how did she possibly manage, and actually when you came down to it, wasn't it just the teeniest bit low-life? Well, that's what they were thinking, I swear.

Miss Miller was at some of those leaden little parties, and she always gave me the impression that she was so overcome at being included in the august gatherings that she might just leave the ground and soar off into the blue if one more partner uttered one more kind and gracious word to her. A sort of female Uriah Heep, so 'umble it'd make you puke. I disliked Miss Miller and until this moment I hadn't realized how much, and with what good reason. The two-timing viper was a certainty to have set her cap at Pa and driven him out of his mind with desire. Those quiet, demure ones are the ones to watch. Then I began to wonder if Ma knew about her. Maybe I should ring and tell her where the danger lay. But I then figured that the reason they'd sent me up here was so they could talk things over and get things out into the open. Maybe Pa had moved in with Miss Miller already. . . .

In spite of my familiarity with the eternal triangle situation (I've watched enough television and read enough magazines to know a fair bit about marriage breakups and the reasons thereof), I couldn't help feeling sorry for Pa. That Miss Miller was a type I knew very well. Still waters. I wondered how deeply he was involved with her.

Then I wondered if I really wanted to know. The whole thing was a problem that I would rather not have to face. It would suit me best if my parents telephoned again and said they'd decided to stay together for the sake of the children, namely me. From my reading I know that lots of people do that. I thought I could even cope with the fights and silences as long as we didn't have to think about divorce anymore. The prospect was so depressing.

I finished my apple and wandered back to the ford. It was too late in the afternoon to visit Mr. Cooper again. No doubt he'd be busy with his pre-dinner nap, but I made a firm decision that tomorrow I would march up to the Pelican homestead and find out which Jem Cooper, about a hundred years ago, had been fond enough of a person called Ann Bird to give her a brooch engraved with a promise of "Ever," and why it had been buried in an old mine shaft for a hundred years until I found it there.

Ann

THE track that leads from Pelican Creek to the town of Gulgong must be one of the most scenic in the world. Certainly it seemed so to me as I jolted along on Mr. Prew's wagon with Jem riding beside us. From each gully we passed came the echoing sounds of pebbles and sand in metal rockers and the noise of men working and children shouting. From each gully it seemed swarms of birds with brilliant plumage flew to greet us. It was the most happy day of my life, and I shall always treasure it.

Mr. Prew bumped along beside me on the wooden seat, holding the reins in one hand and a very impressive stockwhip in the other. The handle measured in length more than he did himself and its thong, plaited strips of hide, was twice as long again, twelve feet I would say. He waved it above the horse's rump in a ferocious and threatening manner, but I never saw it touch, and the old horse ambled along contentedly, seemingly unaware of the terrible threat.

"Bullocky," he muttered cryptically when he saw me looking at the whip, but he said no more so I had to guess that a bullock driver had given him the stockwhip.

Or perhaps sold it to him, or made it for him, or whipped him with it! It was certainly not the weapon one would expect a mild baker to flourish.

We passed several small settlements on the way. Groups of canvas tents, some with sheets of bark laid across the top to form a stronger roof, and bark huts smaller even than ours.

So much bark had been stripped from the trees for building that the countryside was bare and forlorn, with dead stumps and dying gums, but the willows in the gullies were green, and every miner we passed gave us a cheerful wave, which Mr. Prew returned with such a vigorous shake of his stockwhip that at times I feared we might overturn.

"You managed to persuade your father, then?" Jem shouted to me above the clatter of the horses' hooves and the rattle of the cart's huge wheels.

I smiled at him and nodded, not wishing to lie about the matter and hoping that my father *would* be persuaded when the moment I had chosen to persuade him came! Jem seemed satisfied, and I put Father out of my mind, more fully to enjoy the sunny splendor of the day.

I found Mr. Prew's dray a more comfortable conveyance than either of those we had traveled in from Sydney. First there had been the fancy carriage that Father had bought for his trip to Bathurst, a flimsy thing that could hardly carry the three of us and all the luggage that poor Mama had insisted on bringing. *I* would have chosen to travel by the train across the Blue Mountains. It follows, I believe, as nearly as possible, the tracks made by the first explorers who went there, and it has an exciting zigzag section where the train goes back and forth to climb the steep hillside, and an impressive viaduct across the Nepean River at a small town called Penrith. The railway stops short of the town of Bathurst because there is no bridge yet built across the wide river Macquarie, but the trip as far as that would have been so much more speedy and comfortable than the jolting one we had until the moment came when, as Father put it, we had a spot of bad luck! As spots go, it was immense. First the flimsy vehicle hit a large boulder and one of the wheels came off. *That* caused the axle to break, and *that* caused the poor horse to stumble and hurt his leg. All of which caused my father to fall into such a rage that he abandoned the carriage where it lay beside the road, sold the horse on the spot to a passing traveler, and I fear would have sold Mama and me if anyone had made him an offer! Fortunately the boulder that had caused our downfall, or at least the horse's (we were walking beside at the time, as it was on an uphill stretch), was close to a staging inn for Mr. Cobb's coaching service, and after lengthy argument Father was able to obtain seats for us and space for our luggage all the way to Pelican Creek.

I swear my mother did not open her eyes once during the entire trip. It was terrifying! And splendid! In Father's carriage one had the feeling of being in direct contact with the road, such as it was, but in the commercial coach, slung on leather springs, with four great horses pulling it at full speed, we were flung about as if we had no weight at all, and hurtled through the bush at a great rate. The driver, or "jehu" as Papa called him, cracked his whip all the time and shouted at the horses to urge them on. I longed to be up front with him, with branches springing at us as we passed and the wind and the rain joining in the battle to prevent us from going through. Instead I had to crouch inside the stuffy coach with Mama taking small, shuddering breaths beside me. It was not until we had completed the journey that I realized they were prayers she had been uttering as we were flung about; she always claimed that it was the strength and sincerity of those prayers that brought us to our destination in safety. *I* imagine that even more gratitude should have been given to our jehu! And if God were to have the credit for the safe ride in the coach, surely he should be given the blame for wrecking our fine carriage and injuring our poor horse into the bargain.

At last we came to the busy town of Gulgong.

It was a big place, with people bustling about or standing in groups to talk as if it were the day of the fair. There were many shops with their goods displayed in windows and on the road outside, there were hotels, some built of slabs, and we passed one very grand newly built inn, a proper post office, and horses and carriages and bullock drays and dogs in the street. It was a long time since I had seen such activity, and I was so pleased when Mr. Prew at last "whooed" his horse to a stop and we alighted.

He left the horse and cart under the tall gum tree that stands in the street in front of the Queensland Hotel, and Jem tied his horse to the hitching post nearby. Mr. Prew was to see to the horses while Jem and I had the day to ourselves, so we left him there and set off up the street to explore.

We had passed through Gulgong on our way to Pelican Creek in the coach, of course, but I had been too occupied to take notice of it. What with Mother's praying and the coach's headlong dash and my bonnet flying off my head each time we bounced off a stone, I had little time to enjoy the scenery. But today, strolling along with Jem, I was able to appreciate what a fine town it was.

And what shops there were! The Times Bakery was much bigger than Mr. Prew's small establishment, and each of the blacksmith's forges we passed was much blacker and much hotter than Wm. Ryan's. We passed the Crystal Fountain, where they sell hot drinks and spiced beer, and the circulating library, where I hung back a little, but Jem pulled me along.

"No time today. That father of yours will murder us both if I don't have you back before dark." And he was right, of course. In fact, there was a good chance that Father might murder us both even if we *were* back on time! We hastened on past *The Guardian* newspaper office (NEWSPAPER AND GENERAL PRINTING OFFICE, CARDS, BILL-HEADS, POSTERS, CIRCULARS, PROGRAMS, RECEIPT BOOKS PRINTED AT SHORTEST NOTICE). Mother would have been interested in that, as her father is a printer back home in London. But of even more interest to me, and a source of sadness, was the sight of the sign DR. KELLY'S CONSULTING CHAMBERS. SURGEON AND ACCOUCHEUR. By the time she was ready to admit to needing a doctor, my mother was too weak to travel, and she had been too aware of our poverty to ask that one be sent for.

The general store cheered me up, with chairs and ladders hanging from posts, and bolts of cloth piled on boxes, brooms and ax handles stuck in barrels, straw hats on a table beside heaps of doe-skin trousers and rows of sturdy working boots. It was like a vast Aladdin's cave, but again Jem pulled me away, past the colonial wine and dining rooms, which smelled enticing, to a much smaller boardinghouse that advertised meals at one shilling and board at sixteen shillings a week. He put his head around the doorway.

"Is it all right if we come for a meal in an hour, love?" he called, and a muffled voice from the rear answered that it would be, so we hurried on and into the Bank of New South Wales. I waited while Jem went to the counter. Soon he joined me with a great smile on his face and a packet of money that he carefully placed in his wallet.

"Now," he said, taking my arm again to steer me back along the street. "We shall complete the business I began when I was last here. This is the good part of the day."

For myself, collecting money from a bank would be the best that any day could possibly offer, but I was too happy to argue and meekly followed him into the tobacconist's shop (FANCY GOODS, JEWELRY, TOYS, PATENT MEDICINES, AND PERIODICALS).

There a very mysterious transaction took place, with Jem looking very closely at an object the man behind the counter gave to him, then taking out his wallet and paying for it, then having the man wrap it carefully in some paper and placing it almost reverently in the pocket of his jacket. They exchanged satisfied nods, and off we went again. This time it was to another tobacconist, this one advertising fancy goods and a book department! I hoped that Jem's business here would take longer so that I might browse for a while among the books.

Inside the shop he produced his wallet again, took a five-pound note from it, and held it out to me. "Ann Bird, I want you to buy yourself some books with this," he whispered, while the man at the counter stretched his neck to hear our conversation.

"No, Jem. Put it away at once!" I hissed. "Thank you, but no. I cannot do that." I looked about me at the rows of new and tempting volumes. For me *this* was the real Aladdin's cave. "Well, I suppose it would be reasonable if you were to buy me one of them. But just one. And you must choose it. Yes, that would be quite acceptable, I think."

I moved away to let him choose, and he followed me, still whispering frantically while the tobacconist extended his neck farther still. "No! I will not choose! And not just one! You must spend all of this, and if you need more I have it, but I will not choose. Here." He thrust the money toward me again and I waved it away and laughed.

"Why will you not choose? Pick me out one of those you have read and enjoyed the most, and I shall enjoy it too."

As soon as I said it I *knew*. And I could feel tears of shame behind my eyes. Jem said nothing, but held the money out to me still. I took it and walked across to the shelves of books, blinking quickly in case the shopkeeper saw that I wept.

It was so difficult to choose. I sought first the books that had been in my grandparents' home in Bloomsbury and snatched *The Complete Works of Shakespeare* as if grasping the hand of my dearest friend. Artemus Ward had been a favorite of Grandpapa, but he was not here. Miss Austen and Mr. Dickens were, and I had to take *Emma* and *Pride and Prejudice*, *David Copperfield* and *The Pickwick Papers*. I fancied a dictionary, but they had none, so I chose *Ivanhoe*, and *Vanity Fair*, and *Wuthering Heights*.

I gave the change to Jem, claiming that there was too great a number of books for me to make more choices today and thus making sure that we should return for more!

Then we walked back to the boardinghouse, where a table had been set for our meal. After cooking for so long myself I had all but forgotten what properly prepared food could taste like. Bowls of Windsor soup to begin with, then mutton chops, tender and succulent, with vegetables separated on the plate, not all of a hotchpotch as mine always seemed to be. The apple pie was stodgy and thick, just as I like it, and to follow we had a pot of coffee, which neither of us had tried before and which neither of us much enjoyed.

We were too intent upon eating to speak during the meal, but we smiled a lot and I frequently patted my precious bundle of books that occupied the chair beside me. When we had finished making faces over our coffee cups, I pushed mine aside and tried to thank Jem for his generous and most welcome gift.

He would not allow me to. "Listen to me, Ann Bird. As you guessed back there, I cannot read nor write. There was no schooling where I come from, only poverty and hunger, and I've had no opportunity of learning since then. But you *can* read and write, and it surely must be the most precious gift you can have, apart from freedom and good health. So treasure it, enjoy the books I bought you, and think about the others that I want to buy you in the future. Because I want to give you every single thing your heart can yearn for, Ann Bird. I truly do."

"I shall teach you, Jem," I promised. "I shall teach you to read and to write. I know I can do it, if we can only persuade Father . . ."

"You had no trouble persuading him to let you come today! Your father will be no problem to us at all, you'll see."

That was a timely reminder! I had completely forgotten about Pelican Creek in the excitement of busy Gulgong, and the dread must have shown on my face, because Jem asked anxiously, "What is it? Are you not well?"

I decided that what might follow could come in its own good time; there was no point in suffering in anticipation, so I smiled that I was perfectly well, and we left the boardinghouse to stroll down the street again. Jem was unsettled. I knew he had something to say to me. A proposal of marriage was too much to expect, although I should certainly have accepted at that moment! We passed Mr. Prew's cart, now laden with goods to take back with us, but there was no sign of the owner, so we walked farther along until we were in open country. Jem led me to a small stream with a willow, much like our own at the ford, and we sat together in its shade.

Then he took from his pocket the small parcel wrapped

in shiny paper. He took my hand and placed the parcel in it.

"I told you I had business to transact in Gulgong. Well, this is part of it. This is for you, Ann Bird," he said. "Will you wear it for me? 'Tis only the first of my offerings to you, but it comes with my love. All my love."

I opened the parcel and inside was the golden nugget Jem had brought to the hut for me the night my father had turned him away. It had been professionally polished, and in the center was set the diamond that had belonged to Jem's father. It was the most beautiful object I had ever held. I turned it over and saw that the back was flat with a pin attached to it, forming a brooch, and on it was carefully engraved:

ANN

BIRD

JEM

EVER

I pinned it to my shawl. "Thank you, Jem. I shall wear it with such joy and such pride . . ."

He put his dear arms around me and patted me for a moment, then said briskly, "Come along now, it must be time. Old Prew promised to take care of the horses, so we'll not keep him waiting."

I thought it would be very pleasant to stay just a little while longer. Perhaps fifty years. But he took my hand and lifted me to my feet, and we hastened back to the Queensland Hotel, where Mr. Prew was waiting by the dray.

Sally

THE prices at the cattle sales were slightly higher than Uncle James had expected, and Aunt Bess's friend had heard from another patient in the hospital that there were rain clouds gathering on the other side of the ranges. This report was not confirmed of course, might only be a bit of gossip, a case of wishful thinking, Aunt Bess took trouble to tell us, but we all snatched at the tiny strand of hope, and it was a cheerful dinner table that night.

Except for me. Annie was still snitty with me and tossed her head when we passed, just like one of her stupid horses. *I* was still snitty with her, too, but I was determined not to ask *her* for any more information even if I never found out about the stone on the shaft.

I was worried about my parents, too, to be honest. Why I hadn't realized about Dad's affair earlier I couldn't imagine. When I thought about it, he'd been showing all the signs for months, and on the few occasions I'd seen Miss Miller so had she, when I came to think about it. I wondered if poor Ma knew. Well, she would by now, of course, since they'd decided to split, but had she known for ages and not let on so that I wouldn't be upset? Had Pa known that she knew? Why hadn't she been able to confide in me? I swear I would have helped her.

In my sympathy for my deceived maternal parent I glared around the table. There was Cooper, stuffing his face with food, eyes swiveled around to catch the weather report on the television in the corner. There was Uncle James, stuffing *his* face while he caught up with the news in the current copy of *The Land* that was propped up against the salt and pepper grinders. And there was Davey, long since finished his own meal, openly scavenging on everyone else's plate to see if there was anything left that he could polish off. Aunt Bess, who'd cooked and served their meal, washed and ironed the clothes they wore, made the beds, cleaned the house (with a little help from Annie and me), who'd obviously been a slave to those three tyrants all her married life, was talking away cheerfully with no one listening to her, least of all her husband and sons, and offering them more apple crumble! Honestly, men make me sick, although I must say Uncle James gave no signs of having a roving eye, Cooper, apart from the spindly Jezebel at the dance, seemed to prefer to spend his time with animals rather than people, and Davey's only interests seemed to be eating, making lists, and mourning lost hours at the town dump.

They weren't such a bad lot, but the thought of being married, and being at the mercy of someone as selfish as just about all the men I knew, was a bleak thought.

Aunt Bess caught me eyeing her menfolk. "Sal darling, isn't it great news about the rain? I know we haven't had any here yet, and maybe we won't, but it's so good to know that there is a cloud *somewhere*, isn't it? I mean, if they have a good fall over Mudgee way, at least the creeks might rise a bit, mightn't they, James?"

Uncle James did his "Hmm? Hmm" act and Aunt Bess

nodded in a delighted way, just as if he'd gone to the trouble to listen to her and answer. Maybe it was enough for her after all those years of marriage. I felt so miserable I could have plonked my face in my plate and bawled.

"You know, I think it might be an idea if you telephoned home tonight, dear. Just to see how they are, and tell them that you're well. . . ."

I jumped up at once. Good old Aunt Bess nattered on ". . . sure to be someone at home by now. And do ask if you might stay a few extra days. . . ."

"Ma! School goes back on Monday. She can hardly stay a few extra days, for God's sake. . . ."

"Annie dear, I do wish you wouldn't blaspheme. If Sally wants to stay and her parents don't mind . . ."

"*She* mightn't mind. *They* mightn't mind, but I'm telling you someone who will mind! Old Mother Weston, that's who. She'll mind, old Mother Weston will. It'll be detentions for the whole entire term if Sally comes back late. Old Mother Weston can't *stand* people coming back late."

"Very well, dear, you've made your point. Just ring home, Sally, have a chat. Give them our love. And Annie, Miss Weston is your principal and entitled to some . . ."

Respect, I guessed, as I scooted along to Uncle James's office to telephone in private. It wasn't going to be easy, breaking the news to Ma about Miss Miller, but she had to know about her. Anyway, it might be some comfort for her to know that I knew about it and sympathized. I counted eleven *par-parps* before the receiver was picked up, and a weary voice said hello.

It was my father! I'd thought he'd moved out, so I'd expected poor Ma to answer. Obviously he'd driven her from the marital home and ensconced the malevolent Miss Miller in her place. I was tempted to hang up, but curiosity stopped me.

"Hi. It's Sal. Where's Ma, please? I want to talk to

her." I knew I sounded rude and I didn't give a damn.
"She's not here. How are you, darling?"
Don't darling me! "Well, where is she, then? I thought *you* were the one was leaving."

There was a costly silence. I hate trunk calls, but I didn't feel inclined to help him out, so I waited; something in the way of explanation was needed here. Finally he muttered, "I'm sorry, Sal. I thought she would have told you. Your mother moved out the day after you left."

"Where? Grandpa Sloane's place?"

Another interminable silence, then he told me. I listened without uttering a word. I *couldn't* have uttered it even if I'd been able to think of anything appropriate to utter. I told him I'd be back on Sunday night's train, and he said he'd meet me. I hung up and slumped in Uncle James's big chair and stared at the pile of bills that littered his desk.

My mother had run off with Mr. Pearson from her office! Pa had known about it for ages, and *he* was the one who'd been trying to save me from the knowledge! I felt as if a bomb had exploded right inside my stomach. I wandered back through the kitchen and helped myself to some more apple crumble on the way and told Auntie Bess that her love had been returned. Because of my shock it hadn't even been *sent*, but she wasn't one to delve too deeply into things. She realized, bless her, that I was a trifle shaken, so sent me, excused from washing up, early to bed.

I couldn't sleep for ages; even my toes were curled up like a parrot's around a perch. I did all the relaxation techniques I'd ever read about and none of them helped—they couldn't even unravel my toes, let alone get me to sleep—so I hauled out the brooch again and tried to focus my mind on Ann Bird and Jem Cooper. *Ever.* It was reassuring to know that *someone* had loved forever in this world.

It was one of the worst times of my life. Nights in the country are so dark! And quiet! Apart from an occasional moo or baa, or the whoofling of a horse or the rattle of a dog chain, there was nothing, and I was used to city noises. By the time daylight came, my ears and eyes were as tense as my toes, straining to hear a distant motor car or see a glimmer from the streetlights in town about fifteen miles away!

It was almost ten o'clock when I woke up and Aunt Bess brought me breakfast in bed. Most of the work I usually helped with had been done by then, of course, and I felt guilty, but the way I was, I wouldn't have been much use among the horses and bulls anyway. At the first sideways look from Ugly I would probably have just lain down and let him kick me to pieces, the bulls likewise.

It was a cloudy day, had been a cloudy night, hence the darkness more extreme than usual, and although no one mentioned it, there was a waiting feeling in the house. They thought the rain might be on its way at last.

Cooper was going over to Pelican to fix the fence near the woolshed, so Aunt Bess suggested that I go with him and return some cake tins she'd borrowed from Mrs. Dobson. I suspect it was her way of taking my mind off my mother's defection, and I wondered how long she'd known. But I didn't want to talk about it, so I didn't ask but meekly followed Cooper out to the truck with my load of cake tins and some bottles of preserved peaches that Aunt Bess thought might come in handy for Grandpa Cooper.

"That woman's all heart! And clever with it. Just look at them peaches will you? Beautiful!" Mrs. Dobson exclaimed as she stacked the tins in her cupboard and admired the perfect symmetry of the fruit in the bottles. I had to admit they were works of art, with each slice slightly overlapping the next, all the same size and color.

Almost too good to eat, but I was glad to see that although Mrs. Dobson could admire an artistic arrangement, she didn't hesitate to slip an old knife under the lip of the lid to unseal one of the jars, and empty the contents into a dish as the basis of a pie for lunch.

Mr. Cooper was awakened from his post-morning-tea nap, and he and Cooper went off to start on the fence; I sat in one of the big old Windsor chairs and prepared vegetables while Mrs. Dobson made pastry.

She was willing to talk, but only on subjects that she chose herself, so the going was heavy. We covered the rainfall, or lack of it, for the past six months, and the plans and hopes that were swinging on the clouds that had gathered overnight. Mrs. Dobson's grandson was even postponing his wedding until they'd had a good fall on his property. Because if they didn't, he'd have to go to the city to find another sort of job and leave fewer mouths to feed.

"Always been battlers, the Dobsons," she boasted. "Good people, but. Bit religious for my taste some of the older ones, Bible bashers, you know, God botherers, but good people. And hard workers. You fancy a nice cup of tea, love? Be a while till dinner's ready and the men come back."

I'd been keeping myself going on raw beans and pea shells, so was grateful for a little something, and while we had it, I delved into Mrs. Dobson's past with very satisfying results.

"Came with the gold rush, my family did. The Dobsons too, both families were here by the early seventies. My great-grandfather was the baker over there on the hill where they all settled. Had a little shop, and him and my great-gran baked bread for all the miners. Marvelous woman she must have been. Helped him with the baking and the shop and had nine kids. Seven survived, and all did well. Old baker Prew bought a bit of a farm when the gold finished, and since then there's always been Prews in the area. Dobsons too, come to that."

"Did you say the Dobsons came with the gold rush as well?

"Finish off that cake, would you, love? Yes, old man Dobson was the butcher. See, always been some connection with food for me, hasn't there? They came with meat on carts first of all, selling off the cart to the miners and that. Then they set up a shop to sell from. Wasn't much of a shop by today's standards, I s'pose, none of your freezers and electric slicers then. They hung the carcasses outside the shop, under the veranda roof, and on Saturday nights there were tables out there with great slabs of meat for sale, mutton and beef. Musta been a great picnic for the flies, eh?"

The slice of cake with the tiny black currants in it began to look less appetizing. "It's a wonder they didn't all die," I said, ashamed for taking so much for granted.

"Lots of 'em did," Mrs. Dobson answered cheerfully. "But lots didn't. We had none of this refrigeration nonsense when I was a child, even. I well remember my grandma laying down beef. She'd cut it into strips and rub salt into it. Then put it into the sun to dry and pack it into barrels against the time when she needed some and the men weren't killing. Mind you, she lived out west a fair way. No butchers' shops where she was then. She had a great way of curing bacon, too. I used it for years when this family was young. Always had a nice side of bacon hanging in the pantry. Then he got all this newfangled electric stuff installed, and it was a plastic bag o' this and a sealed container o' that. I like a few of the good old ways myself."

She dragged the oven dish with its sizzling roast out

of the oven and turned the meat over, then surrounded it with potatoes and pumpkin chunks and set it back to cook again.

"Funny all the oldest Cooper boys being christened Jem, isn't it, Mrs. Dobson?" I said as I took our cups and plates over to the sink to wash. "You would have known a few of them, I imagine."

"Knew *all* of 'em. The Coopers were here a good thirty years before the gold, mind. They were squatters. Two brothers rode out here and decided what land they wanted, then one stayed to guard their claim while the other went back to Sydney to pay the license fee—it was ten pounds then, and they had to pay a yearly levy for the stock they grazed on it."

"So why didn't one man just claim the lot?" I would have.

"Well, they had to buy so many animals per acre or whatever it was. It was the law, see. They could only take as much land as they could afford to stock."

"I'm really more interested in the gold miners, Mrs. Dobson. I've . . . er . . . heard about, read somewhere about, someone called Ann Bird. Do you remember your grandmother mentioning a family called Bird at all?"

Mrs. Dobson untied her minute pinafore. I could have used it for a doll's outfit a few years back when I was into dolls. She gave me a conspiratorial grin and took my arm.

"Come with me," she said. "I'll introduce you to her."

Ann

THE daylight was beginning to fade as we pulled up outside the baker's shop in Pelican Creek. Jem had ridden ahead for the last part of the trip so that we should not be seen together, and was waiting to lift me down from the dray.

I quickly transferred my brooch from the outside to the inside of my bodice and hurried inside to speak to Mrs. Prew.

"Calm yourself now, ducks." She nodded and winked and smiled so busily I could scarce make out what she was saying. "I sent young Barney to speak to your father, like you said. He's the pick o' my lot for that sort o' thing. No one can't hardly understand what young Barney says at the best of times, so there's no means of getting what you'd call a clear message out of him. But he said your Pa seemed satisfied. Had a happy day then, did you?"

I assured her that I had, purchased a loaf of bread, thanked Mr. Prew for taking me and for looking after the horses, tossed a quick wave to Jem, and set off for home with my bundle of precious books and a conscience heavy with guilt!

I heated water for his wash and had his meal prepared by the time Father came in, but he sat down first to question me. He was quite beaming with pride, and I did hope that I could manage to give him sufficient explanation without completely destroying his happy mood.

"Well, my dear," he said, smiling and rubbing his hands together, "did you enjoy your trip to Gulgong with the squatter's wife? Eh?"

I did wish that I had young Barney Prew's ability to so muddle the conversation that no one even *expected* to have any sense out of me. But I knew my father well enough to know how to answer.

"I enjoyed the trip very much, thank you, Papa, but—"

"And what manner of person is she, the squatter's wife?"

"I am sure that she is a very amiable and kind pers—"

"Amiable and kind, of course, befitting someone of her rank and station."

"She is not royalty, Papa. And as it happened I did not spend the day in her company."

"Well, even part of the day . . . a very gracious lady I am sure. And you had a satisfactory meal in Gulgong?"

"Oh yes, Papa." At least I was telling the clear truth now. "I had the most *delicious* luncheon."

"And did she speak to you of her son?"

"No, Papa. I told you . . ."

"Ah well, there is time. It is sufficient for the moment that she has acknowledged our presence here. No doubt there will be further invitations. Yes. A very gracious lady. *He* is known to me of course, the husband. Pleasant enough chap. Mind you, he has been extremely lucky here, every opportunity . . . the lad said there was business to attend to on her behalf."

"Yes, Papa, Mr. Prew did attend to some business for her." He had brought back extra sacks of flour for her, I knew.

"I thought that he or the son might have accompanied you. Surely she did not drive herself?"

"Oh no, Papa. Obviously the baker's lad has given you a misleading message. How annoying, particularly when I was so careful to give it clearly to his mother! I did not travel to Gulgong with Mrs. Cooper."

"Ah, I see, of course. Not the done thing . . . show too much friendship so early in the court— so early. No. Much more discreet this way."

"Father, I did *not* go to Gulgong *with* Mrs. Cooper. Mr. Prew was doing an errand for her, and I went with him."

There, now he had the truth. But of course the truth was not what he wanted. I had noted when Mother was alive that Father would accept any story so long as it added to his self-esteem. It suited his vanity to believe that I had been invited to accompany Mrs. Cooper to Gulgong, and that she had taken me to lunch and bought me books. It seemed to me to be a kindness to allow him to continue to think thus, since I *had* told him the truth of the matter, so I served him his supper, he ate it happily, and we never discussed my trip to Gulgong again.

While my father dreamed in cheerful expectation of my marriage to Charles Cooper, I happily spent part of every day in the company of Jem Brady, doing some dreaming of my own. I felt guilty at first, since I had never deliberately deceived Papa before. Well, I had in fact, quite frequently, but only in little things. But this time I knew so strongly that he was wrong and I felt the time with

Jem to be so precious, that I was willing to take the chance of being found out.

It was no easy matter to arrange our meetings. Father was so reluctant to go to work that all the other miners were well into their day before he left the house. And he insisted on returning for lunch, although every other miner worth his salt took a pannikin of food with him to eat. He often came home early these days as well, disheartened by his failures and eager to be off to the hotel to buy some comfort there.

So my day was chopped into small pieces, full of anxious and furtive activity. Immediately after breakfast I would announce that I had to visit Chan Lee's garden to purchase some vegetables for our meal. Father disliked being in the hut alone, so I knew that when I left, he would go too, and I could rely on his being at work or giving advice to the other diggers for at least an hour. Then I would pick up my skirts and dash across the ford to Jem's mine, whistling our tune loudly as I went, circle around it and return to the willows to wait for him. And to do that without an immense loss of dignity is no easy matter! I *am* lucky to have Papa to take care of the dignity department in our lives; he does it so well and I do it so badly!

We dared not go to a more secluded spot; that would *really* cause a scandal were we found out, but the ford was not very busy when the men were at work, and our willow gave us shelter.

We would sit there, my hand in his, my head against his shoulder, and he would tell me such stories of Ireland that I breathed its sweet air and it filled me with joy. We would plan our future there, fishing in the river and walking in the woods of Dromore, living in a tiny house near Kenmare with six little Jems and five Ann Birds to delight our hearts. And there would be no more famine in Ireland and no more sorrows.

Then I would bring out one of my books from the pocket of my apron and he would read to me. I am sure there could be no quicker pupil than my Jem. He was so eager to learn and I was so eager to share the joys of reading with him that our time fled away and the hour to go home and prepare Father's lunch would be upon us. Fortunately Papa never noticed the absence of all the fresh vegetables that I was supposed to be buying from Chan Lee!

Sometimes, when we had the time, Jem and I would walk by the creek, in the opposite direction from my father's mine of course, and it was there on a sandy spit that I gave him his writing lessons. He would willingly have bought writing materials, but I liked to teach him his letters in the sand. There were two rocks standing close together. We would sit on these, after selecting sticks of just the right length and thickness, and Jem would follow carefully the shapes of the words I wrote. This way I was able to tell him many things that I would hesitate to say aloud, and after his careful reading and copying of them, we could rub them out so that no one would ever be able to know what I had said.

One day, when we were working thus, there was a flurry in the water nearby. Jem jumped up and ran to the stream, waded in and in a moment came back to me carrying a good-sized fish that was still flicking frantically. He put it away from the water on a dry rock, and picked up his makeshift pen to write again.

"There's your dinner, Ann," he said in a very casual manner, waiting for me to show signs of amazement at his feat.

"Thank you, Jem," I replied calmly, happy to hear that the poor fish had stopped its leaping and could now be presumed dead. I was disappointed at his brutality, and it must have shown in my voice, because Jem hastened to explain.

"The fish is food, Ann. Can we afford to be sentimental about it? 'Tis an old fish, a very old creature indeed. He's lived a good life. He was tired, ready to go. And then he came upon this clever little fish trap, didn't he, and he thought, 'Ah, what a fine rest I'll be having in there. How peaceful it looks.' So he swam into the little trap, and was waiting there for me to pick him up. Delighted to be providing a hearty meal for the likes of us."

I smiled, won over again. "What do you mean, a fish trap? Did you set it?"

"Not me. Tribes of black men who lived here set it up years ago," he explained, and took me over to see.

It was ingenious. A large fallen tree had been wedged between the banks of the creek, with small branches crisscrossed beneath it and held in place by an interlacing of poles. I could see that small fish could swim easily through the net, but larger ones, such as Jem had just caught, would be trapped in the branches and held there until they were retrieved.

"There's only a few of us know of this one," Jem warned me, "so don't be talking about it. Enough fish get caught in here to give us a decent meal from time to time, and you, Miss Ann Bird, are now one of us, a member of the Pelican Creek Fish-Eating Club."

He wrapped the fish in a bundle of leaves, bowed low, and presented it to me. I hurried home with my booty, and it certainly was a "decent meal," and better still, Papa did not ask where it came from.

Papa did not, in fact, ask very much at all these days, and I asked little of him, so we seldom spoke. He was fast becoming what is known as a "Lushington" and often came staggering home at night long after the rest of the township was asleep. Each hotel keeper is obliged by law to keep a light burning outside his establishment from sunset to sunrise, but how my father managed to make his way to our hut after he had left that helpful glow I cannot imagine.

I would lie awake listening for him and praying that he would not have an accident, for then we should have no money coming in at all. The amount he made from his mine was small enough, but the thought of doing without it was quite frightening. I realized in those dark hours just how much I had taken for granted all the comforts we had back in London, and how Mama must have worried and suffered before she died. I also feared his being injured because I doubted my ability to look after him as patiently as I had cared for her. Papa showed no signs of being the uncomplaining, submissive sufferer that Mama had been. I could foresee sharp battles and hard-fought wars were he to be injured and I to nurse him.

My prayers must have been heard, since Father never did fall on his way home from the hotels. Well, fall he may have, but he was never badly injured. Our greatest problem was poverty. There was no other female of my age in the community, although several lived on the surrounding farms. They were lucky, having work to do. I begged Papa to allow me to seek employment so that I might earn some money to help us out. I felt sure that Mrs. Cooper, being so "amiable and kind," would employ me as a housemaid. But he refused to discuss the matter. No daughter of his . . . how dare I . . . position in society. . . . I did not pursue the matter, knowing that he still saw me as a future mistress of Hampshire, not as a skivvy there. Besides, I might find it even more difficult to arrange meetings with Jem were I to be working at the big homestead.

I always wore my nugget brooch, inside my bodice of course, out of view, and when I was most anxious I would rub it gently with my fingers, a charm, a talisman. I had cause to rub it so often that I was sure that my father must think I was suffering from a severe and aggravating itch!

One day when Jem met me by our willow he was plainly worried. He took my hand and led me to our place, then, not looking at me, began to speak.

"'There's rumors, Ann," he said. "People passing through are telling of another strike, farther west. Some of the men are for heading off to be in at the start and stake a likely claim. There will be a great number moving on from here."

I dreaded to hear his next words. How could he think of leaving me when he *knew* how worried I was, when he *knew* of my unwavering love. With one hand I hurriedly groped for my brooch and began to polish it. My other hand was clutched in Jem's and even though I tried to remove it, he would not let me go.

"I want you to know, so that it might not come as such a great shock to you when it happens. Because it will, Ann. Nothing surer."

I chewed at my bottom lip to stop the stubborn thing from its trembling, and blinked my eyes until my eyelids ached. But I would not beg him to stay.

"Do you understand what I say to you, love?"

I nodded, blinked, chewed, and polished so energetically that I must have appeared seized by convulsions, because Jem stared at me, startled.

"Don't be so upset. I had no idea it would bother you so much."

I could cheerfully have pushed the stupid fellow into the creek, but I shook my head to show that nothing was bothering me in the slightest degree.

"I mean, if he chooses to go—and the men drinking with him last night are sure that he plans to—then surely you would choose to stay here. I mean, I thought, I hoped that you would."

So it was my father he was talking about. Making plans to go on to the next goldfield, leaving me behind. I was silent, so thankful that it was not Jem who was leaving that the prospect of being abandoned did not disturb me in the least.

"You will stay, Ann? I promise to look after you. We can be married, and I'll catch you fish and bring you gold and take good care of you, better care than your father ever did."

"If he goes, I shall not go with him," I promised. "But it may be only a rumor."

He agreed that rumors were always blowing through the settlement, and we parted.

That evening when I asked my father if he had heard of a new gold strike farther west, he shrugged and shook his head and hastened away from the hut. And as usual I lay in my bed and prayed that he should not fall and be injured on his way home in the dark.

Sally

MRS. Dobson led me out of the kitchen, along the flagged veranda, and into the main house. She stopped before the fireplace in the big sitting room and pointed to the painting that hung above the mantel.

"There she is. The original Ann Bird Cooper. Mrs. Cooper, meet Miss Sally Matthews."

"Sarah, actually. How do you do." Formality seemed to be required in the presence of this formidable woman! Her dark hair was piled smoothly on top of her head; she wore a black dress, all tucked, with a high neck and a lace collar closed by a big cameo brooch. And her steady, dark brown eyes seemed to be able to see right into my brain!

So this was the owner of the nugget brooch. She certainly wasn't beautiful, but so strong! She had the look of a person who could do anything if she set her mind to it. If this was their ancestor, I could understand where the Coopers' steady determination came from, to say nothing of their pigheadedness!

"There's a few photographs of her about too, if you want to look at them." And she shoved me down in the old velvet grandfather chair by the fireplace and handed me some photograph albums. "The men'll be in for their meal soon. I'll call if I need any help." Then she toddled back to the kitchen.

I began with the oldest-looking album, and sure enough, there she was in a bridal group, looking as if she'd been included by mistake and was in fact just passing by and not approving too much of the goings-on! White trains and veils and bouquets and ribbons didn't suit Ann Bird at all. The bridesmaid looked a lot happier than anyone else, and even she looked ready to weep! The bridegroom had moved, so that his face was a palish blur; the best man looked fit to sob, as did the older couple, who I guessed were the groom's or the bride's parents. Mind you, in just about all the old photographs I've seen, everyone looks as if they're being told extremely sad news by the photographer. Looking happy in those days was obviously not the done thing.

The next snap was more cheerful. Here was Ann Bird posed on the same red-velvet chair that I was sitting on right now, on her knee a dear little baby in a white smock, and leaning against the chair a small boy in a sailor suit, with another one in the same sort of outfit sitting on the floor beside her.

Cooper came clomping in at that moment to call me for lunch.

"See you've met Great-great-grandmother." He patted her shoulder gently, as if in greeting. They were friends, obviously, and I took a closer look at Cooper. He had the same dark-brown eyes, the same straight look.

"Tell me about her."

"Come and eat. I'll tell you about her then."

"I knew her well," Mr. Cooper said between mouthfuls of Mrs. Dobson's mighty roast dinner. "She was almost ninety when she died. That was in 1944. I would have been . . . ah . . . let's see now . . . born 1912 . . ."

"You were thirty-two, Grandpa. It was the year Dad was born, and she was eighty-eight."

"You were at the war, Mr. Cooper, along with all the young men from around here." Mrs. Dobson turned to me, with a serving fork full of sliced lamb and a serving spoon ready to heap my plate again. I let her, only so that the conversation might not be interrupted. "Ridiculous it was, our own men over there fighting in Italy and wherever, and we had Italian prisoners of war here working their farms for them! Always struck me as being stupid. Now, if a woman had been in charge, they'd have all stayed in their own countries . . . saved the trouble of moving them about!"

Even though I felt there was something wrong with her reasoning, I knew what she meant. Fortunately old Mr. Cooper was well launched in his reminiscences of his grandmother.

"Very strict old lady, she was. Had taught school when she was younger, you know, and my word, she could keep us young ones in our place! No nonsense when Grandma was around, but she was good fun. I remember when I was a child she used to take me for walks with her. Had a regular route you know, down to the creek and across by the ford. Sometimes we'd take a little picnic and have it there beneath the willow. I really think she was at her happiest there. Mind you, it is a peaceful, lovely spot."

"I know," I said, "I've been there." And I felt myself, oh hell, blushing, and rushed on, hoping Cooper hadn't noticed. "Did she come with the gold rush?"

"Another place we used to visit a lot was that big old gum on the far slope, where the creek winds back again. There's an old elm tree there . . ."

"Gold rush? . . ."

". . . and you know, I've just remembered, it's funny how things come back to you once you start thinking. Another favorite visiting place for Grandma was that old shaft where you fell in, young Sally."

"And wasn't that a terrible thing to happen to you just as you arrived, you poor thing. I said to Mr. Cooper, I said . . ."

"She shouldn't have been charging about there in the middle of the night. We had to go to no end of trouble to hoist her out again. Wasn't easy, I can tell you."

"I wasn't . . ."

"Funny, you know, she never took a picnic there."

"Where's that, Mr. Cooper?"

"The shaft. He's telling us about the old mine shaft." I decided not to have any more lamb.

"No, we never picnicked there. Nor played games, come to think of it. She made us sit quietly by the mine shaft as if we were in a church, but we had a lot of fun in the gully by the creek. Yes . . . she was a grand old lady, Grandmother Ann Bird."

I dashed backward and forward between the kitchen and the dining room, helping Mrs. Dobson to clear the plates and bring in the peach pie and a big bowl of cream, hoping not to miss any of Mr. Cooper's reminiscences and vowing seriously to get stuck into a diet as soon as I was back at school. When we were settled down again attacking our wedges of pie, I jogged his memory once more.

"So she lived here all her life did she, Mr. Cooper? Grandmother Ann Bird?"

"Of course she didn't. Came here with the gold rush, didn't she, Grandpa? About eighteen seventy-one-ish?"

"Well, *my* great-grandma was here first. She and her husband, Mr. Prew, they were just about the first to arrive, they were. Mind you, they only had to come from over Bathurst way. . . ."

"She used to tell us that she came with her parents from England in eighteen sixty-nine. Father a restless kind of chap by the sound of him, couldn't settle to anything in England, so the mother's parents paid their passage out to Australia. . . ."

Mrs. Dobson chortled happily. "Well, the government paid the passage money for my folks! The first Prew out was a poacher I think, and his wife was up for stealing cheese. . . ."

"You really did begin early in the food game, Mrs. Dobson. Just a tiny slice, thanks."

"Mind you, we don't talk about it much outside of the family. Them being, you know, convicts. Not many people like to have convicts in the family closet. Worse 'n skeletons, my old mum used to say."

"It's not like that these days, Mrs. Dobson. People are *boasting* about the convicts in their closet where I come from!"

Mr. Cooper plowed on. "The idea was, I imagine, for him to take up land or start a business, but when gold was discovered here, he dragged Ann and her mother across the mountains to make his fortune. Terrible life for a woman, you know. She'd been used to so much better, the mother, a London house and servants, and she wasn't strong. Died soon after they arrived, I believe. Her grave is by the big gum over there. You know, Cooper."

"The elm tree. Yeah. They usually buried them near the house and planted a sapling to mark the spot."

"Well, if you're not going to help me out by finishing this off then, I'll just have to clear it away."

Mr. Cooper and Cooper helped her out; honestly I don't know where the old man and that skinny boy put it! Then we made tea and I had to wean the two of them from a fascinating discussion of various treatments for tick infestation back to Ann Bird.

"Jewelry? Good heavens, no, she wasn't one for jewelry, and anything the mother had brought out with her the father would have sold, I imagine, or gambled away. No, she was very poor when they were married, in money terms only, you understand. In everything else she was wealthy beyond anyone else around here. She was a fine scholar and teacher and she'd read just about every book you could name. She'd started a little school here for the miners' children before the government set up schools, and they let her keep the job of teacher when the local school began. Gave it up when she married my grandfather, of course. Full-time job managing things here."

"Tell her about Kenmare, Grandpa."

"Ah yes, that was a strange thing, wasn't it? All her life Grandmother spoke about Kenmare as if she'd come from there and missed it sadly. It's a town in Ireland, but I expect you know that, you youngsters know so much these days. She talked of Moll's Gap, the Lakes of Killarney, the mountains they call Macgillycuddy's Reeks, the walks by the river, and the sea about there. All of us children loved to hear her tell tales about Ireland; it seemed she had a different lilt to her voice when she spoke of it. . . ."

"I'd better get back to that fence in a minute. . . ."

"Now, just be still there and have another cup of tea, young Cooper." *Dear* Mrs. Dobson.

"So what was so strange about that? Maybe she *did* come from Kenmare."

"No, my dear. Grandmother came from Bloomsbury. Never had been anywhere near Kenmare in all her life. My grandfather took her overseas for a trip once, you know they used to do the grand tour in those days—by ship of course, the real thing. He offered to take her to Ireland, since she obviously loved it so much, but she wouldn't go. She refused flatly to go there, said she couldn't bear to see it, her memories were enough for her. Memories! And she'd never been there at all! It *is* a bit strange, isn't it?"

It was strange. She was emerging as a very odd person, this Ann Bird. Yearning for a country she'd never seen. Sitting quietly by a mine shaft where she'd lost a brooch her husband had given her, as if she were mourning for it.

Old Mr. Cooper was beginning to nod over his teacup. Mrs. Dobson jerked her tiny head in his direction and smiled. "Wonderful, isn't he? I can't force a decent bit of food into him, eats like an ant, but just let him have a snooze for a while, and he'll be fit for anything again. You help him to his bed now, will you, young Cooper, and I'll see to this."

The clearing and washing up was going to be gargantuan, but she was so *frail*! "You have a rest too, Mrs. Dobson, *I'll* see to this. No honestly, I love washing up."

Cooper, suddenly stricken with a fit of laughing, almost dropped his grandfather to the floor, but managed to retrieve him at the last moment and led him out of the door. Mrs. Dobson wouldn't hear of me doing the lot, thank goodness, but was happy to have some help.

"Got a dishwasher affair there, but only use it when we've got a crowd."

Four was crowd enough for me, but we did the dishes together manually. Mrs. Dobson, although fragile to look at, had a core of solid adamantine. Cooper flashed a grin and a wink as he went past on his way back to the fence.

"Give you a whistle when I've finished," he called. "Have fun, you two."

"Lovely boy," Mrs. Dobson cooed, tippy-toed and bottom-up at the sink. She wouldn't let me wash, and I could see her drowning in there if she had to fish too deeply for a fork. But on the other hand, reaching up to get the plates from the draining board wouldn't be too easy either, so I let her do what she wanted (as if I had any choice) and watched carefully in case rescue was needed.

"Image of his gran he is, the old mad one, I mean."

"Mad? Was she mad?"

"In my book she was as mad as they come. Mind you, I was only a young girl when I knew her. Came here as housemaid, I did. Rest of them thought she was Christmas, but I reckon she was a shingle short, myself."

There was a footstool by the stove, so I dragged it over and tried to set it up beneath her wobbling toes.

"Why don't you try standing on this. Make you higher."

She gave me a cranky glare and pushed it away. "Don't need to be any higher, managed pretty well up to now without that, thank you very much, and you left a smear on that plate."

She didn't actually say it, but I distinctly heard a "Miss Know-it-all" in there, so I hauled the stool back and redid the neglected plate.

"What do you mean, a shingle short?"

"Well, shingle short's putting it a bit mildly I'd say. When I first met her, I thought she was just that, nutty as a fruitcake, you know, but as I got to know her better I reckon she was as mad as a meat ax. I mean, she'd got everything she could ever want here hadn't she? Mind that knife, it's a sharpie. They've always been well-off, the Coopers. Better off then than they are now, in point of fact, but with all the money they had, old Grandma Ann Bird used to drive me mad with her economies."

I grabbed the broom to sweep the kitchen floor and just beat Mrs. Dobson to it. Believe me, that woman is a *dynamo*! Not to be outdone, *she* grabbed another cloth and set to polishing the front and top of the stove.

"I'd like to get this done while it's hot. Cleans better then. Yes, the old girl was a funny one. Had a contraption for making candles she brought with her when she married Mr. Cooper. With all the electricity we got here, she used to insist on making these smelly candles out of mutton fat and alum I think it was. Had me tearing up old bits of woolen cloth to make the wicks, and she'd pour the stuff into these tin molds on a tray, and when they were set she'd fill the shelves in the pantry with the rough old things. Mind you, it was pretty hard finding a bit of woolen material that she hadn't set aside to work on! She used to sit and mend the boys' clothes until there were more patches than cloth!"

"Sounds as if she liked to be busy, then." That character trait alone should have ingratiated the old woman with Mrs. Dobson; surely she'd love a bustler like herself, a fellow toiler.

"Busy! Never! She didn't like being busy! What she liked best was taking one of them old books she was always nose deep in and sitting out under gum trees and willows and beside old mine shafts, and reading until her eyes must've been ready to give out. No, she didn't like being busy. It was saving money she was into. Take the soap!"

I looked around. No soap.

"You'll never believe this, but she even used to make soap! Stuff used to stink out that pantry along with the candles. More mutton fat, and other caustic stuff, all poured into a big flat tin lined with a bit of old linen. I'd have to put up with it laying about on the table there until it was set, then she'd use my best knife to cut it into blocks."

"Couldn't you just get rid of it and pretend it'd been all used up?"

"You stupid or something?"

No, just mad as a meat ax, silly as a two-bob watch, a shingle short.

"She'd have known. No flies on Grandmother Ann Bird there wasn't. Add to which, Mr. Cooper, her husband that was, was so proud of her, used to make them all use the stuff, *and* the candles as well. Every one of those kids had to take a candle up to bed with him at night. The trouble I had getting them out of the habit after she died! Him up there still insists I keep a box in the pantry in case we have a blackout. I reckon he'd still be using his granny's if I hadn't been firm with him."

"What else did she do that was crazy?"

"That's enough, isn't it? I came to work here in nineteen forty, when I was a girl of eighteen, and she made my life a misery till she pegged it four years later."

I realized then that it was not the economies but the head-on collision of two strong characters that had caused Mrs. Dobson's dissatisfaction. Grandmother Cooper was the hardier battler of the two, and with her candles and her soap and her mendings she had won.

"But she made Jem Cooper happy, didn't she, when she married him?" I asked slyly, hoping to show Mrs. Dobson that some women could be just as tough as some others.

She flattened me with no trouble at all. "Married who?" she said, whirling a fistful of steel wool around the oven top. "*Who* did you say she married?"

"Jem Cooper. Her husband." The man who gave her the brooch, who wanted to take her to Ireland, the grandfather of that sleepy old darling upstairs who wanted to take the candles to bed only you wouldn't let him. The oldest son of the family, which he would have had to be to stay on living in this house after he was married. *That* Jem Cooper. Surely I didn't have to explain.

"No," she said, carefully examining a hot plate for signs of grime. "He wasn't named Jem. It was when they had children that it started, the business of calling the oldest son Jem. She insisted on it. And he said the oldest girl was to be called Ann Bird, after her, see. So little Annie over there, she's Ann Bird, too."

"You mean her husband wasn't called Jem?"

"No, love, what on earth made you think that? His name was Charles."

Ann

IT was the nineteenth day of September, and there had been heavy rain, but now the sky was clear and the earth smelled sweet.

I sat on my bench beneath the gum tree, close by my mother's grave. The small tree that Charles Cooper had planted there was looking healthy and strong, and I was glad that poor Mama was at last at peace in this land that had been so alien to her.

I had in my hands Miss Austen's *Emma*, one of my favorites among the books my dear love had obtained for me, and was pondering on the possibility of starting up a school for the children of the community. If the parents were willing to pay two shillings a week, surely a paltry price for the richness education would bring to their children, then I could manage very well, and perhaps put something aside for the rainy day that I was sure would come. Ten shillings a week would be better, of course, but would I be happier to have two pupils at the most, at ten shillings a week, or perhaps twenty at two? I wished that I had chosen a book of economic theory with some of Jem's gift; there must be some clever logical law that would solve my problem.

I set my thoughts aside for the moment and returned to Miss Austen. I know precisely the page I was reading: Emma and Harriet were calling on Mrs. and Miss Bates.

The sun was warm upon my back and I was content.

Suddenly down the hill from the settlement a young lad scrambled, shouting to the men who were working at the puddling machine.

"Help! A fall! Help!"

Immediately I knew.

I gently laid my book on the bench beside me and stood up. Then I ran more swiftly than I had ever run before, and I was at the top of the rise before the men had left their wagons and horses and their gold and begun to follow.

I had no need for directions, but sped along the track, with the men panting along behind me. We skirted the township and flew across the ford, took the narrow track up the other side of the hill, and then we saw the anxious group of men and women standing at the top of Jem's mine.

As I approached, I could tell by the demeanor of the crowd that there was no hope for him. Some of the women were wailing loudly, with their shawls over their faces, others quietly sobbing, their ready grief for others being part of their own desolation in this poor place.

I could not weep. I stood back and watched as men climbed carefully into the shaft and tried to shovel the earth away. Dust was settling around them and those who climbed out to let others attempt a rescue were filthy and mud coated.

No one paid any attention to me save Mrs. Prew, who came to stand beside me. She gently took my hand in hers. " 'Twas a rock fell on the poor lad," she murmured. "All this rain weakened the soil."

At last I managed to speak. "Perhaps there was no one down the mine when it collapsed?"

I yearned for agreement, but they all knew. Jem had been speaking to one of the men at the top of the next shaft a moment before he entered his own. That man had seen and heard the rocks and earth come loose and tumble down the pit.

Kind Mrs. Prew pointed the man out to me. I walked across and questioned him. He thought my words were sprung from aimless curiosity and answered brusquely, so that I longed to be able to scream my grief out loud and tell them all that I had more cause than they to mourn the terrible accident. Instead I thanked him for his information and stepped as close to the pit head as I was allowed. It was clear Jem must have perished. A solid floor of mud and rocks had settled about ten feet from the top. It was unreasonable to hope that he could have survived either the weight of the fall, or the lack of air that would ensue.

I stood beneath a tree, numb with my grief. I would have entered that dark hole eagerly and clawed at the mud with my own bare hands had I thought such efforts would help. The men were doing their best, no one could do more, and it was not for lack of helpers that the rescue was doomed. Miners had abandoned their own diggings to come; all the shopkeepers were there, plus a raggedy group of children who romped and played uncaring, as children do. Even in my misery I thought how beneficial schooling would be for them.

Mr. Cooper was there with his son; they dug and worked beside the miners as long as there was yet some hope. Young Charles bowed in my direction when they arrived and later came to stand beside me. I think he knew something of my feelings. He was very kind.

"You do realize, I hope, Miss Shipton, that the young man would have died instantly. There can be no question of his survival under the weight of that earth fall. I tell you this since you may have been acquainted with him, and I would have you be aware that he would not have suffered long. I believe he was a very fine person. I wish I had known him better myself."

"I am obliged to you, sir." And indeed I was. He had offered words of comfort yet given no offence, and I knew that my secret would never be divulged by him.

Later in the afternoon my father came to the hillside. He stood near me, yet far enough away as to be free to speak without seeming to address me. In fact he directed his remarks more to Mr. Cooper senior, since he had always deemed the other miners to be below his station and the Cooper family sufficiently above it to be worth cultivating.

I felt a sudden, rare surge of sympathy for my father. His life was made up of high hopes and deep disappointments. Having been brought up to expect a comfortable life with no effort required on his part, he had acquired no ability to work hard or to accept the responsibility of providing for his family. He had become a sad, failed man the moment fortune ceased to smile on him.

"This is a tragedy. A tragedy, sir," my father said to Mr. Cooper and his son as they stood with bowed heads by the shaft. "The mine was carelessly dug, no doubt; the young man had little experience. . . ."

"There was nought wrong with the mine, sir," replied Mr. Charles Cooper. "It was the freakish rain we had that caused the rocks to slip."

His father touched his arm to silence him and spoke civilly to my father. "It is indeed a tragedy, such a young, strong man. I knew him at the smithy. This country has need of men such as he."

"I also knew him," my father boasted, eager to appear as catholic in his acquaintances as the property owner. "A fine young chap, yes. One feels some gesture is required, as I hear that no further efforts can be expected to recover the . . . the body." He was trying to be considerate of my feelings, but I wanted to tell him, by way of reassurance, that nothing he, or anyone, could say could touch me now, nor ever again.

But I remained silent and he went on.

"Perhaps some small monument. Erected here. To close off the pit in case of further accidents. And also, of course, to serve as a stone to his memory."

"That is a kind and generous thought," Mr. Cooper replied, and I imagined my father's earnings for some time being used to finance his grandiose plans. I saw no need for a memorial. Not in stone, and certainly not paid for by my father. But he was quite carried away by his own eloquence and the approval of the squire.

"Yes," he said, "I envisage a simple slab. With something carved on it, like a proper headstone. Do we know the details of this young man? His date of birth? Family home? There is a stonemason in Gulgong, I believe, who could be commissioned to do the work." He looked about him at the crowd, none of whom were eager to be involved in his scheme.

"His name was Jem," one volunteered finally.

"Brady," added another.

"Came from Ireland," offered a third.

I could have told them so much more. The date of his birth and the place of it, his beloved Kenmare. I could have told them the dreams of his soul and all about his loving, generous heart. But I remained silent, hoping for my father's sake that he would have done and take me home.

He did at last. Having promised to inquire of the next traveler to Gulgong how to go about commissioning a suitable stone.

When we were at last back at the hut, I rescued *Emma* from the bench while Father lit the candles. Then he pleased and surprised me by offering to set a meal himself, which he did, although clumsily. Cold corned beef and a slice of bread satisfied him, and I had no appetite, so our dinner was over quickly.

He did not go to the hotel that night, and I was grateful for his company, although he offered little by way of companionship, leaning back in his chair and tapping the top of his boot with a switch, until I was tempted to knock his hand away. I sat at the table, a candle beside me, keeping my eyes on the pages of my book. Reading nothing; feeling nothing but a cold numbness and unutterable despair.

When it was time to retire to our beds, my father rested his hand on my shoulder, with a touch of his old gentleness. "I am sorry it happened this way, lass," he whispered. "But you do understand, don't you?"

"Yes, Father. I understand." And indeed I did. I understood that I had been deprived of the pleasure of an open friendship with Jem because my father was unable to tolerate his lower social standing. He was saying now that it was really for the best that Jem was dead. No further embarrassments need occur!

"Good girl. I knew you were a sensible girl. He was possibly a worthy enough young fellow. For an Irishman. But it would never have done. I am glad that you realize it. I shall see that he has a decent burial service and a fine tombstone. You mark my words."

Burial services and fine tombstones were nothing to me. Jem was dead, and I was desolate. I gave the dutiful answer that was expected of me.

"Yes, Papa."

"By the way, my dear. You may recall asking me if I had heard of another gold strike farther west? Well, I have made some inquiries, and sure enough, the rumors appear to have some weight. So I think, when I have completed the arrangements for the stone for the young Irishman, we might make plans to move on. What do you think of that, eh?"

I thought nothing of it and told him so. "What home I have is here now, Papa. You go by all means, but I shall remain. I have plans to start a school for the children, and I shall manage."

"Well, we can talk about it later. You are upset tonight, I can see, but things will seem brighter tomorrow, you mark my words. Young people are remarkably resilient."

And he went happily to his bed, having settled all problems to his own satisfaction.

Even alone and in the darkness I could not weep. I lay on my bed, listening to the creatures scurrying about in the rafters and behind the walls of my room, lacking the strength and inclination tonight to clap my hands to frighten them off.

At last daylight came, with its first bluish haze. It is an eerie time of day, before the dawn, when the light is pale and the air is still.

I arose and dressed myself, carefully pinning my beautiful brooch to the *outside* of my shawl this time. Then I crept through the main room and let myself out of the door. My father snored on and did not hear me go.

I walked slowly up the hill, past the township, where no one was yet stirring save for Mr. Prew, whose shutters showed light through. I turned at the creek and stepped slowly and carefully across the flat stones. Even the water was still and peaceable this morning, as befitted a place holding memories of so many tender meetings.

Leaving the creek, I took the path that led to the side of the hill and the grave of my dear love.

There was no dust, as there had been yesterday. The air was calm and quiet. I stood for a while beside him, and silently prayed for the repose of his glowing and beloved soul.

As the light grew stronger, I heard the first sounds of morning activity from the tents farther along the banks of the creek. Soon people would be moving about and I would be seen. I could afford to linger there no longer.

I unpinned the nugget brooch that he had given me, inscribed with our names and the simple pledge of our abiding love.

ANN

BIRD

JEM

EVER

A keepsake he had called it. But I needed nothing to remind me of him. I would never in all my life forsake the memory of my beloved friend.

I held the brooch in my hand, polishing its luster with my fingers. I kissed it reverently one last time. Then I cast it down into the grave.

Sally

SO someone had loved her who wasn't her husband, had promised to love her forever. She'd lost the brooch he gave her down the mine shaft and grieved about it for the rest of her life. And serves her right, I reckon. I jolted along beside Cooper in the truck and hoped that my mother would have something that would make *her* feel guilty as long as she lived for what she'd done to me and to poor old Pa.

"You're very quiet. Want to talk about it?"

"No thank you, Cooper. That rain's holding off."

"It'll come. You leave day after tomorrow. Glad to be going home?"

"No."

"Right."

We drove in silence the rest of the way. I didn't want to talk about my troubles; airing them only brought them more sharply into my mind, and I wanted to be an ostrich for another day and a half. I couldn't talk about his great-great-grandmother either, because I was the only person living who knew that she had been unfaithful to poor Charles Cooper. I had no idea they did things like that in those days! Just goes to show, doesn't it? That guy in the Bible who said there is no new thing under the sun knew what he was talking about.

But Ann Bird hadn't finished with me yet! When we jittered over the cattle ramp and into the yard, Uncle James was waiting.

"Stone's arrived, Coop," he said. "Get the kids to give you a hand, eh?" And then, in his usual fashion, he touched the brim of his hat with a finger in greeting to me and drifted off.

It was an enormous, round, flat stone, far too heavy to be lifted onto the truck, and although I liked Davey's suggestion that we just let it roll down the hill like a hoop, I could see that the results might be catastrophic. So Cooper fixed chains around it and hitched them to the tow bar of the truck, then drove carefully downhill to the corner of the home paddock, with the three of us running along behind hoping frantically that the stone wouldn't come adrift and flatten one or all of us.

He was a brilliant maneuverer, was Cooper, managed to stop the truck just before it was due to hit the fence and just where the stone was closest to the shaft. We all heaved and shoved and finally it came to rest right over the hole, and we all came to rest right on top of it, heavily.

"Well, we shouldn't have any more nutters falling down there," Annie gasped. Then, leering at me. "No carving on this one then, Coop? Sally's interested, aren't you Sal?"

"I'll put the carving on myself, later."

"Still want to know what it is, Sal?"

I could quite honestly say that I didn't. I really didn't want to know any more about their great-great-grand-mother; I thought she must have been a pretty rotten lady, actually. But the fact that I no longer showed any interest made Annie at last ready, even eager, to tell me.

"It said, 'Jem Brady 1850 to 1872 R.I.P.' Mean anything to you?"

It only meant that Ann Bird's lover was called Brady and had, wait a minute, had probably died down that mine shaft. I lay on the brown spiky grass and glared up at the murky clouds as I thought it through.

Jem Brady gets killed in this mine shaft in 1872 and they put a stone on top to mark a sort of grave. The stone cracks, breaks, and finally falls down the shaft, and as it goes it dislodges a rock, exposing the nugget brooch for me to find. So the brooch must have gone down the shaft before the stone was put in place. Unless she dropped it down and poor Jem Brady toppled in while he was trying to retrieve it for her. It beat me, and I had to give up thinking about it finally because my face was getting wet . . . and my arms . . . because holy . . . *wow!* It was raining!

We all jumped up and shouted, and Cooper grabbed me and kissed me quite hard, right on the mouth, and gave me a really solid hug, and then had to hold me up for a while because my knees went weak on me! Fortunately the other two were so busy hooting back up the hill to spread the word that they didn't notice anything, and Cooper and I tossed the chains on to the back of the truck, he saluted the grave of Jem Brady, who should probably have been his great-great-grandfather, and we drove in silent bliss back to the house.

What a night that was! We were all so *happy!* Davey danced around the house singing, "She's not heavy, but she's steady," laughing like a loon as if it was the funniest crack anyone had ever made. Annie was as friendly as anything and offered to play Scrabble, but I didn't feel in the mood. After they'd watched the news and the weather report (hopeful at last) on the television, Cooper came over to where we were sitting at the table embellishing pictures of politicians in the local paper. He suggested a game of poker, so we agreed to that and Aunt Bess joined us and I won eighty-three cents, which made me feel more optimistic about going home. My luck just might have changed for the good. Uncle James opened a bottle of his home brew and we all drank lots of the putrid-tasting stuff and went off at last, happily stewed, to bed.

It was my last full day at the Coopers' and Ann Bird still nudged at my brain.

The horses had to be fed, of course, and once more I reeled about in the mud with fodder flying any place except into the proper bins, and only the thought of rats in the shed keeping me out there. Lucky old Annie didn't seem to be afraid of anything at all, and I suspect she'd known all the time that Ugly was getting the wrong diet and Sam (or was it Buster?) getting no diet at all! None of them had actually *died* while being fed (or not fed) by me, but I guessed they'd all shake hooves and breathe horsey sighs of relief when they knew I'd gone back home.

Davey was right; the rain was steady, the best kind according to Uncle James, so not much work was done. It was Saturday, too—not that weekends made much difference to the Coopers, they seemed to be flat out working every day except for part of Sunday. But this day was easier than most, and after lunch Cooper suggested we go for a walk around the place while he checked a few things out. Annie offered to come with us, but strangely enough both Aunt Bess and Davey required her help immediately with matters urgent and interesting enough to keep her inside the house. I glugged my feet into the old boots, put on a ragged khaki jacket that was hanging on the hook with the others, about fifteen of them, along the wall of the back veranda, and we set off.

We went to the mine shaft first. The stone was still sturdily in place.

"He must have been one of the miners," Cooper said. "I guess he was a friend of hers."

"Because of the Jems," I said. "There's just one thing, Cooper. What year did she marry your great-great-grandfather?"

"Funny you should ask," he grinned. "It used to bother me, too, when I first started to think about it, but it's all right. They were married in 1882. Story is that she made him wait ages before she'd say yes. Stubborn as a mule she was, but he was even stubborner and just wouldn't stop asking. Grandpa says they were the most devoted couple, all their lives, so I reckon Charles didn't mind the waiting."

We wandered hand in hand to the ford and stood for a while under the shelter of the old willow tree.

"I'm glad you came, Sally," he said, nuzzling my hair if you really want to know. "Chance to get to know you better. To be friends."

I told him that friends was all I was prepared to be. Now and probably forever, because I had no intention of ever marrying anyone and going through all that misery.

"That's okay," he nodded, behind my left ear if you care. "I'm in no hurry. For a while. I'm like my great-great-grandparents, they tell me."

"You *look* like her," I remarked. Into his right shoulder, if it's any of your business.

"Ah yes," he murmured, somewhere around my right eyebrow, "but they say I've got his nature."

We left the willows then and crossed the ford and climbed the other hill to the gum tree with the elm beside it.

"And there's my *great*-great-great-grandmother Shipton. There was talk of moving her body to the cemetery years ago, but I'm glad they left it there. It's a quiet, pleasant place to be resting."

I leaned against Cooper's strong arm, filled with joy that he wanted me to be his friend. He was such a *kind* person.

"I like the elm," I said.

"Don't know where they would have got it," he mused. "The only ones growing around here now are in the garden at Grandpa's. Tell you what I thought I might do, dig up a sapling and plant it by the mine shaft. What do you reckon?"

I could feel tears as well as rain on my face.

"Oh, Cooper," I snuffled, "I think that's a beautiful idea. Do it soon and next time I come up I'll help you water it and we can watch it grow."

"You're on," he agreed, and we had to run like mad back to the house because the rain suddenly pelted down and all the countryside was suddenly misty and mysterious and the earth smelled rich and fresh and alive, and I was so glad that I had come here that I just let myself cry right out loud and Cooper didn't seem to mind at all.

Davey met us at the cattle ramp.

"Hey, Sally, your folks have been on the blower again."

And sure enough, each of them had rung and each of them rang again. Ma said over and over that she hadn't wanted it to be this way, but I couldn't imagine which way she *had* wanted it to be, since she was the one who'd taken up with the poisonous Mr. Pearson. I was rottenly glad that she was carrying on so much, because she was most likely ringing from the Pearson piggery and it was his telephone bill that would suffer, so I let her maunder on. She said she hadn't wanted me to be hurt, she really hadn't. I considered that for a bit and decided that she was probably right. She really *hadn't* wanted to hurt anyone I guess, just hadn't taken the time to think it through and see what the consequences would be. I felt sorry for my mother then; she wasn't a vengeful woman, but she wasn't a thinker-through either.

"Listen, Ma," I finally told her, "I don't think I'm hurt all that much. Not so much that I'll never mend, you know? So just hang in there until I'm back and we'll talk then. Okay?"

She really did sound more miserable than I'd ever thought she could. Adultery can't be all that much fun if it makes you feel like that.

When Pa rang I was well in control and told him that Ma was okay. A remark that obviously did nothing to make *him* feel better about things.

"Oh yes, *she's* all right. I've just been speaking to her myself. Your mother's all right. You don't have to worry about her." Very bitter he was, but I knew that neither of them was doing so well and I'd have to put a lot of work in to smooth things along when I got home.

I was beginning to feel more detached about them now. So they were going to get a divorce. Lots of people get divorced. It wasn't *me* having to get a divorce, so I'd just have to stand off a bit and try to make it easier for them if I could. I wasn't sure that I particularly wanted to; they could have told me how things were going a long while ago, given me a chance to get accustomed to it. Given me a chance to study those kids at school a bit more closely and decide how I was going to handle it. As I went back to the dining room to help Annie set the table, I swore that the first person who came up to me at school and said she was sorry to hear about my parents was going to get a freezing-off she wouldn't forget too soon.

My train left early next morning, so as soon as we'd washed the breakfast dishes, I went into my bedroom and picked up the nugget brooch. I gave it a final polish with a clean handkerchief and took it back to the living room with me.

They were all there; Aunt Bess talking, no one listening. Annie was cutting pictures of horses out of *The Land* to paste in her horsey album. Honestly!

Uncle James was standing at the window, gloating over the rain, and Cooper was mending something made of leather that looked as if it went somewhere on a horse. Davey was making a wool ball so that he could optimize his teasing of the cat. A change from horses, at least!

"Listen, everyone!" I shouted in order to gag Aunt Bess. "That night when I fell down the mine, I found something."

That brought them all to attention, and I wished I'd taken time to compose a proper speech, unaccustomed as I am to being listened to.

"It's a brooch, and I think that Great-great-grandmother Ann Bird must have dropped it down the shaft sometime. Anyway, here it is, and it's inscribed from Jem, and Cooper says it was a long time before she married Mr. Cooper, so it's all right. . . ." I felt myself bogging down in treacle, so I finished quickly. "Anyway, I think you should have it, either Annie, because she's Ann Bird too, or Cooper because he's one of the Jems and the oldest son."

They all gathered around me to look at it and exclaim over the inscription, and Annie announced that she really didn't want it. It wasn't her style, she was into diamanté at the moment and really didn't ever think she'd go for gold, but if they wanted her to, she'd put it away and look after it.

Cooper held it for a long time, then he said that if no one minded, he'd like to keep it, that is, if no one felt that anyone else was more entitled to it. He was really keen to have it, I could see, so I was relieved when Uncle James said that of course he should take charge of it, as the eldest son, and later on when he married and moved into Pelican homestead, maybe his wife might wear it.

In memory of Ann Bird.